Robert Ballard

The Solution of the Pyramid Problem

Pyramid discoveries with a new theory as to their ancient use

Robert Ballard

The Solution of the Pyramid Problem
Pyramid discoveries with a new theory as to their ancient use

ISBN/EAN: 9783337405984

Printed in Europe, USA, Canada, Australia, Japan

Cover: Foto ©Andreas Hilbeck / pixelio.de

More available books at **www.hansebooks.com**

THE SOLUTION

OF THE

PYRAMID PROBLEM

OR,

PYRAMID DISCOVERIES.

WITH A

NEW THEORY AS TO THEIR ANCIENT USE.

BY

ROBERT BALLARD,

M. INST. C.E., ENGLAND; M. AMER. SOC. C.E.

CHIEF ENGINEER OF THE CENTRAL AND NORTHERN RAILWAY DIVISION
OF THE COLONY OF QUEENSLAND,
AUSTRALIA.

NEW YORK:

JOHN WILEY & SONS.

1882.

NOTE.

In preparing this work for publication I have received valuable help from the following friends in Queensland :—

E. A. Delisser, L.S. and C.E., Bogantungan, who assisted me in my calculations, and furnished many useful suggestions.

J. Brunton Stephens, Brisbane, who persuaded me to publish my theory, and who also undertook the work of correction for the press.

J. A. Clarke, Artist, Brisbane, who contributed to the Illustrations.

Lyne Brown, Emerald,—(photographs).

F. Rothery, Emerald,—(models).

and—A. W. Voysey, Emerald,—(maps and diagrams).

CONTENTS.

LIST OF WORKS CONSULTED.

Penny Cyclopædia. (*Knight, London.* 1833.)

Sharpe's Egypt.

"*Our Inheritance in the Great Pyramid.*" *Piazzi Smyth.*

"*The Pyramids of Egypt.*" *R. A. Proctor.* (*Article in Gentleman's Magazine. Feb.* 1880.)

"*Traite de la Grandeur et de la Figure de la Terre.*" *Cassini.* (*Amsterdam.* 1723.)

"*Pyramid Facts and Fancies.*" *J. Bonwick.*

GENERAL PLAN OF GIZAH GROUP

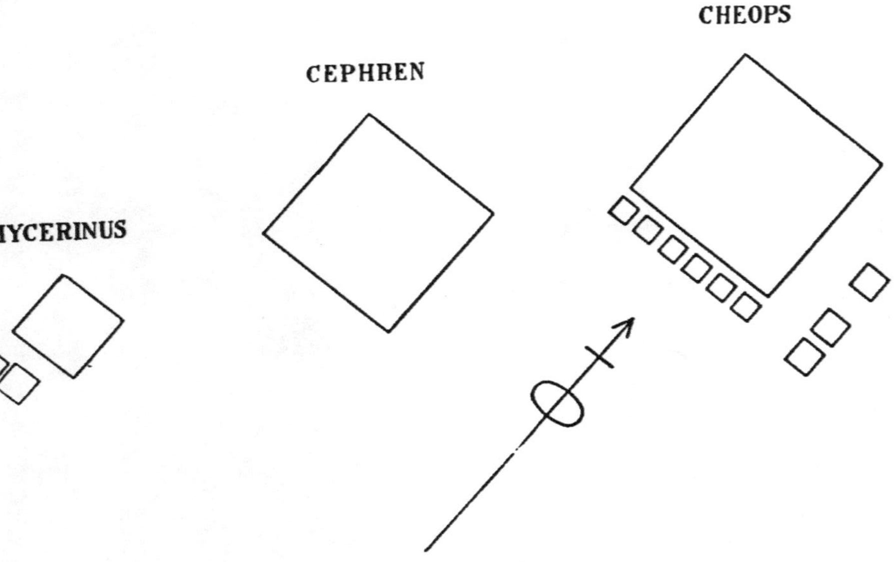

THE

SOLUTION OF THE PYRAMID PROBLEM.

WITH the firm conviction that the Pyramids of Egypt were built and employed, among other purposes, for one special, main, and important purpose of the greatest utility and convenience, I find it necessary before I can establish the theory I advance, to endeavor to determine the proportions and measures of one of the principal groups. I take that of Gïzeh as being the one affording most data, and as being probably one of the most important groups.

I shall first try to set forth the results of my investigations into the peculiarities of construction of the Gïzeh Group, and afterwards show how the Pyramids were applied to the national work for which I believe they were designed.

§ 1. THE GROUND PLAN OF THE GIZEH GROUP.

I find that the Pyramid Cheops is situated on the acute angle of a right-angled triangle—sometimes called the Pythagorean, or Egyptian triangle—of which base, perpendicular, and hypotenuse are to each other as 3, 4, and 5. The Pyramid called Mycerinus, is situate on the greater angle of this triangle, and the base of the triangle, measuring *three*, is a line due east from Mycerinus, and joining perpendicular at a point due south of Cheops. (*See Figure* 1.)

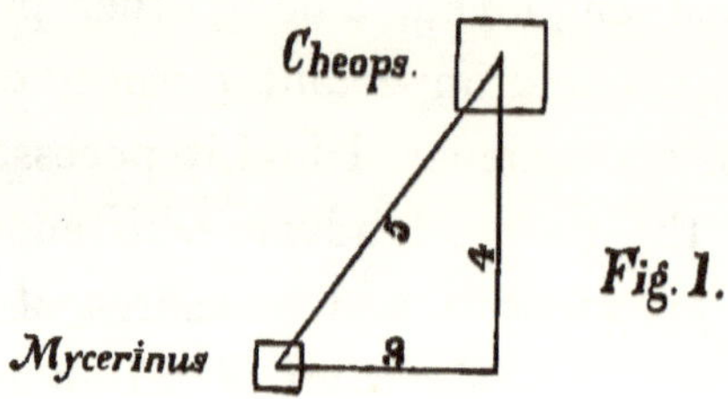

I find that the Pyramid Cheops is also situate at the acute angle of a right-angled triangle more beautiful than the so-called triangle of Pythagoras, because more practically useful. I have named it the 20, 21, 29 triangle. Base, perpendicular, and hypotenuse are to each other as twenty, twenty-one, and twenty-nine.

The Pyramid Cephren is situate on the greater angle of this triangle, and base and perpendicular are as before described in the Pythagorean triangle upon which Mycerinus is built. (*See Fig.* 2.)

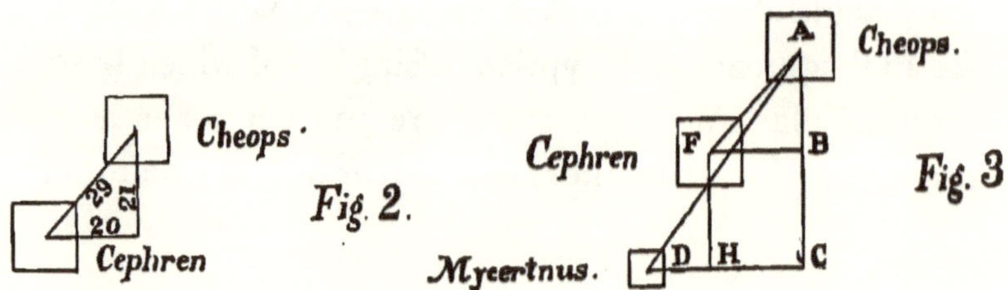

Figure 3 represents the combination,—A being Cheops, F Cephren, and D Mycerinus.

Lines DC, CA, and AD are to each other as 3, 4,

and 5; and lines FB, BA, and AF are to each other as 20, 21, and 29.

The line CB is to BA, as 8 to 7; The line FH is to DH, as 96 to 55; and the line FB is to BC, as 5 to 6.

The Ratios of the first triangle multiplied by forty-five, of the second multiplied by four, and the other three sets by twelve, one, and sixteen respectively, produce the following connected lengths in natural numbers for all the lines.

DC......135
CA......180
AD......225

FB...... 80
BA...... 84
AF......116

CB...... 96
BA...... 84

FH...... 96
DH...... 55

FB...... 80
BC...... 96

Figure 4 connects another pyramid of the group—it is the one to the southward and eastward of Cheops.

In this connection, A Y Z A is a 3, 4, 5 triangle, and B Y Z O B is a square.

Lines YA to CA are as 1 to 5
CY to YZ as 3 to 1
FO to ZO as 8 to 3
and DA to AZ as 15 to 4.

I may also point out on the same plan that calling the line FA radius, and the lines BA and FB sine and co-sine, then is YA equal in length to versed sine of angle AFB.

This connects the 20, 21, 29 triangle FAB with the 3, 4, 5 triangle AZY.

I have not sufficient data at my disposal to enable me to connect the remaining eleven small pyramids to my satisfaction, and I consider the four are sufficient for my purpose.

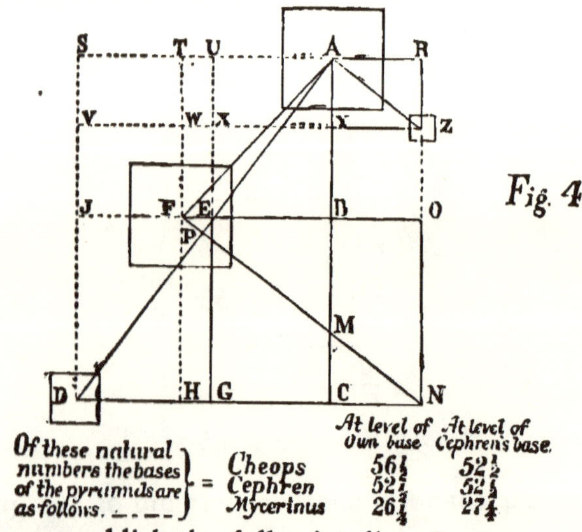

I now establish the following list of measurements of the plan in connected natural numbers. (*See Figure* 4.)

Plan Ratios connected into Natural Numbers.

BY	1	48	48	BC	6	16	96	DC	45	3	135	FB	5	16	80
YZ	1		48	FB	5		80	BC	32		96	BY	3		48
DN	61	3	183	DN	61	3	183	CY	3	48	144	FH	96	1	96
NR	60		180	NZ	48		144	BC	2		96	DH	55		55
CY	16	9	144	PN	61	2·4	146·4	JE	3	24	72	YX	7	9	63
DC	15		135	PA	48		115·2	EX	2		48	AY	4		36
BA	21	4	84	CA	4	45	180	BC	32	3	96	EA	7	15	105
FB	20		80	DC	3		135	EB	21		63	AZ	4		60
CB	8	12	96	YZ	4	12	48	FO	32	4	128	AB	7	12	84
BA	7		84	AY	3		36	OR	21		84	BO	4		48
ED	8	15	120	BA	4	21	84	FT	84	1	84	BC	8	12	96
AE	7		105	EB	3		63	ST	55		55	AC	15		180
VW	55	1	55	GE	4	24	96	VW	55	1	55	ND	61	3	183
FW	48		48	DG	3		72	SV	36		36	NO	32		96
SJ	7	12	84	HN	4	32	128	BJ	45	3	135	PA	48	2·4	115·2
SU	6		72	FH	3		96	AB	28		84	AZ	25		60

The above connected natural numbers multiplied by eight become R.B. cubits. R.B.C.

(Thus, BY, 48 × 8 = 384).

Plan Ratio Table.—(*Continued.*)

GX 2 144 } 72 DG 1 72	GU 5 180 } 36 DG 2 72	EO 37 111 } 3 AY 12 36	SR 61 183 } 3 RZ 12 36
SU 2 72 } 36 SV 1 36	HW 144 144 } 1 DH 55 55	HT 36 180 } 5 DH 11 55	FH 96 96 } 1 FE 17 17
TW 36 36 } 1 TU 17 17	FO 8 128 } 16 OZ 3 48	DA 15 225 } 15 AZ 4 60	EA 105 105 } 1 EF 17 17
SR 61 183 } 3 RO 28 84	JB 45 135 } 3 BY 16 48	AC 15 180 } 12 CN 4 48	WH 144 144 } 1 HG 17 17
YW 20 80 } 4 AY 9 36	FW 48 48 } 1 FE 17 17	YV 15 135 } 9 AY 4 36	TH 180 180 } 1 HG 17 17
MY 9 108 } 12 ZY 4 48	AC 20 180 } 9 CG 7 63	VZ 61 183 } 3 ZO 16 48	
AC 9 180 } 20 CH 4 80	EA 35 105 } 3 AY 12 36	EU 84 84 } 1 FE 17 17	
NZ 12 144 } 12 ZA 5 60	CY 3 144 } 48 YZ 1 48	CA 5 180 } 36 AY 1 36	

The above connected natural numbers multiplied by eight become R.B. cubits. R.B.C.

(Thus, GX 144 × 8 = 1152).

§ 2. THE ORIGINAL CUBIT MEASURE OF THE GIZEH GROUP.

Mr. J. J. Wild, in his letter to Lord Brougham written in 1850, called the base of Cephren seven seconds. I estimate the base of Cephren to be just seven thirtieths of the line DA. The line DA is therefore thirty seconds of the Earth's Polar circumference. The line DA is therefore 3033·118625 British feet, and the base of Cephren 707·727 British feet.

I applied a variety of Cubits but found none to work in *without fractions* on the beautiful set of natural dimensions which I had worked out for my plan. (*See table of connected natural numbers.*)

I ultimately arrived at a cubit as the ancient measure which I have called the R.B. cubit, because it closely resembles the Royal Babylonian Cubit of ·5131 metre, or 1·683399 British feet. The difference is $\frac{1}{600}$ of a foot.

I arrived at the R.B. cubit in the following manner.

Taking the polar axis of the earth at five hundred million geometric inches, thirty seconds of the circumference will be 36361·02608—geometric inches, or 36397·4235 British inches, at nine hundred and ninety-nine to the thousand—and 3030·0855 geometric feet, or 3033·118625 British feet. Now dividing a second into sixty parts, there are 1800 R.B. cubits in the line DA; and the line DA being thirty seconds, measures 36397·4235 British inches, which divided by 1800 makes one of my cubits 20·2207908 British inches, or 1·685066 British feet. Similarly,

36361·02608 geometric inches divided by 1800 makes my cubit 20·20057 geometric inches in length. I have therefore defined this cubit as follows:—One R.B. cubit is equal to 20·2006 geo. inches, 20·2208 Brit. inches, and 1·685 Brit. feet.

I now construct the following table of measures.

R. B. CUBITS.	PLETHRA OR SECONDS.	STADIA.	MINUTES.	DEGREES.
60	1			
360	6	1		
3600	60	10	1	
216000	3600	600	60	1
77760000	1296000	216000	21600	360

Thus there are seventy-seven million, seven hundred and sixty thousand R.B. cubits, or two hundred and sixteen thousand stadia, to the Polar circumference of the earth.

Thus we have obtained a perfect set of natural and convenient measures which fits the plan, and fits the circumference of the earth.

And I claim for the R.B. cubit that it is the most perfect ancient measure yet discovered, being the measure of the plan of the Pyramids of Gizeh.

The same forgotten wisdom which divided the circle into three hundred and sixty degrees, the degree into sixty minutes, and the minute into sixty seconds, subdivided those seconds, for earth measurements, into the sixty parts represented by sixty R.B. cubits.

We are aware that thirds and fourths were used in ancient astronomical calculations.

The reader will now observe that the cubit measures of the main Pythagorean triangle of the plan are obtained by multiplying the original 3, 4 and 5 by 360; and that the entire dimensions are obtained in R.B. cubits by multiplying the last column of connected natural numbers in the table by eight,—thus—

		R. B. CUBITS.
DC	3 × 360 =	1080
CA	4 × 360 =	1440
DA	5 × 360 =	1800

or,

NATURAL NUMBERS.			R. B. CUBITS.
DC	135	× 8 =	1080
CA	180	× 8 =	1440
DA	225	× 8 =	1800

&c., &c.

(*See Figure* 5, *p.* 18.)

According to Cassini, a degree was 600 stadia, a minute 10 stadia; and a modern Italian mile, in the year 1723, was equal to one and a quarter ancient Roman miles; and one and a quarter ancient Roman miles were equal to ten stadia or one minute. (*Cassini, Traite*

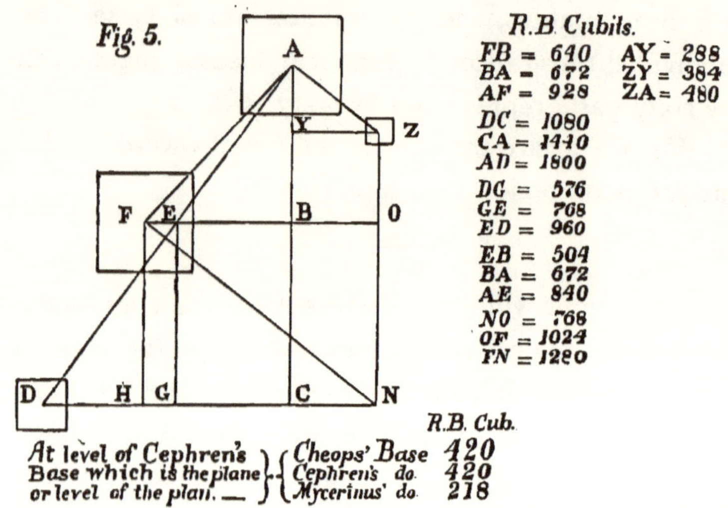

de la grandeur et de la Figure de la Terre. Amsterdam, 1723.)

Dufeu also made a stadium the six hundredth part of a degree. He made the degree 110827·68 metres, which multiplied by 3·280841 gives 363607·996+ British feet; and 363607·996+ divided by 600 equals 606·013327 feet to his stadium.

I make the stadium 606·62376 British feet.

There being 360 cubits to a stadium, Dufeu's stadium divided by 360, gives 1·6833 British feet, which is the exact measure given for a Royal Babylonian Cubit, if reduced to metres, viz.: 0·5131 of a metre, and therefore probably the origin of the measure called the Royal Babylonian cubit. According to this measure, the Gïzeh plan would be about $\frac{1}{1011}$ smaller than if measured by R.B. cubits.

§ 3. THE EXACT MEASURE OF THE BASES OF THE PYRAMIDS.

A stadium being 360 R.B. cubits, or six seconds—and a plethron 60 R.B. cubits, or one second, the base of the Pyramid Cephren is seven plethra, or a stadium and a plethron, equal to seven seconds, or four hundred and twenty R.B. cubits.

Mycerinus' base is acknowledged to be half the base of Cephren.

Piazzi Smyth makes the base of the Pyramid Cheops 9131·05 pyramid (or geometric) inches, which divided by 20·2006 gives 452·01 R.B. cubits. I call it 452 cubits, and accept it as the measure which exactly fits the plan.

I have not sufficient data to determine the exact base of the other and smaller pyramid which I have marked on my plan.

The bases, then, of Mycerinus, Cephren, and Cheops, are 210, 420 and 452 cubits, respectively.

But in plan the bases should be reduced to one level. I have therefore drawn my plan, or horizontal section, at the level or plane of the base of Cephren, at which level or plane the bases or horizontal sections of the pyramids are—Mycerinus, 218 cubits, Cephren, 420 cubits, and Cheops, 420 cubits. I shall show how I arrive at this by-and-by, and shall also show that the horizontal section of Cheops, corresponding to the horizontal section of Cephren at the level of Cephren's base, occurs, as it should do, at the level of one of the courses of masonry, viz.—the top of the tenth course.

§ 4. THE SLOPES, RATIOS, AND ANGLES OF THE THREE PRINCIPAL PYRAMIDS OF THE GIZEH GROUP.

Before entering on the description of the exact slopes and angles of the three principal pyramids, I must premise that I was guided to my conclusions by making full use of the combined evolutions of the two wonderful right-angled triangles, 3, 4, 5, and 20, 21, 29, which seem to run through the whole design as a sort of dominant.

From the first I was firmly convinced that in such skilful workmanship some very simple and easily applied templates must have been employed, and so it turned out. Builders do not mark a dimension on a plan which they cannot measure, nor have a hidden measure of any importance without some clear outer way of establishing it.

This made me "go straight" for the slant ratios. When the Pyramids were cased from top to bottom with polished marble, there were only two feasible measures, the bases and the apothems;* and for that reason I conjectured that these would be the definite plan ratios.

Figures 6, 7 and 8 show the *exact* slope ratios of Cheops, Cephren, and Mycerinus, measured as shown

* The "*Apothem* is a perpendicular from the vertex of a pyramid on a side of the base."—*Chambers' Practical Mathematics, p.* 156.

on the diagrams—viz., Cheops, 21 to 34, Cephren, 20

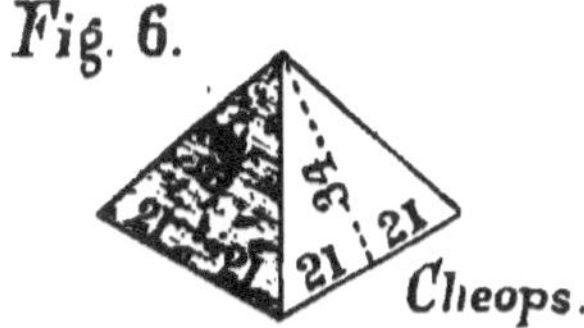

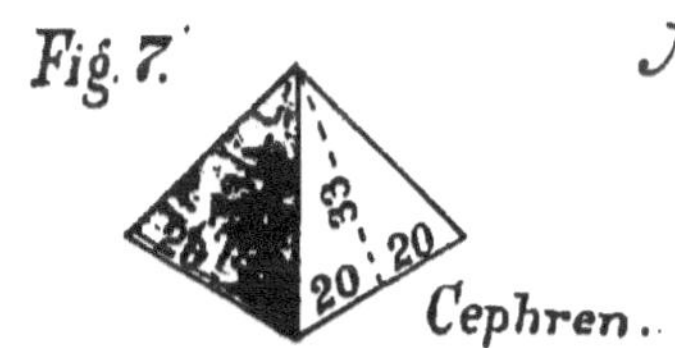

Note. The Ratios of Bases to Altitudes are very nearly as follows, viz:-

Cheops	33 to 21 or 330 to 210
Cephren	32 to 21 or 320 to 210
Mycerinus	32 to 20 or 336 to 210

to 33, and Mycerinus, 20 to 32—that is, half base to apothem.

The ratios of base to altitude are, Cheops, 33 to 21, Cephren, 32 to 21, and Mycerinus, 32 to 20: not exactly, but near enough for all practical purposes. For the sake of comparison, it will be well to call these ratios 330 to 210, 320 to 210, and 336 to 210, respectively.

Figures 9 and 10 are meridional and diagonal sec-

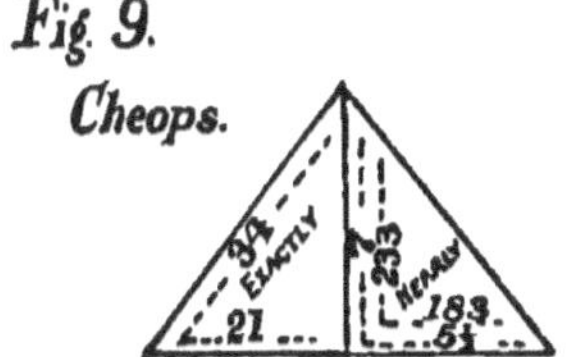

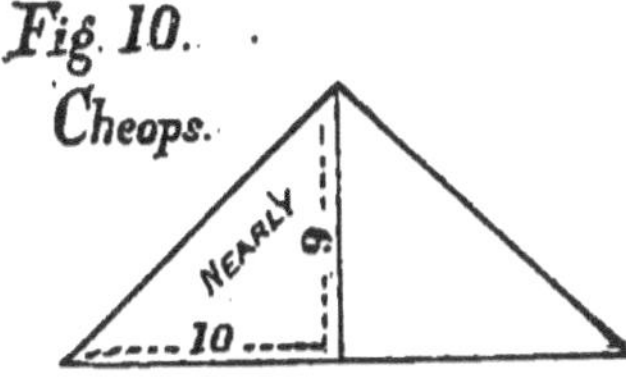

tions, showing ratios of Cheops, viz., half base to apothem, 21 to 34 *exactly;* half base to altitude, 5½ to 7 nearly, and 183 to 233, nearer still (being the ratio of Piazzi Smyth). The ratio of Sir F. James, half diagonal 10 to altitude 9 is also very nearly correct.

My altitude for Cheops is 484·887 British feet, and the half base 380.81 British feet.

The ratio of 7 to 5½ gives 484·66, and the ratio of 233 to 183 gives 484·85 for the altitude.

My half diagonal is 538·5465, and ratio 10 to 9, gives 484·69 British feet for the altitude.

I have mentioned the above to show how very nearly these ratios agree with my exact ratio of 21 to 34 half base to apothem.

Figures 11 and 12 show the ratios of Cephren, viz.,

half base to apothem, 20 *to* 33 *exactly*, and half base, altitude, and apothem respectively, as 80, 105, and 132, very nearly.

Also half diagonal, altitude, and edge, practically as 431, 400, and 588.

Figures 13 and 14 show the ratios of Mycerinus, viz.,

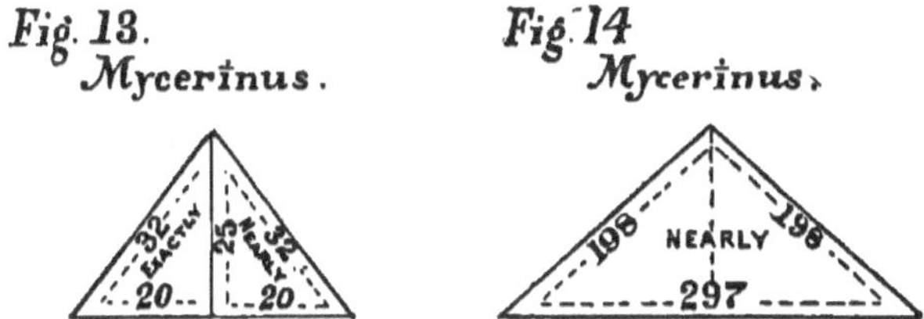

half base to apothem, 20 *to* 32 *exactly*, and half base, altitude, and apothem respectively, as 20, 25, and 32 very nearly.

Also full diagonal to edge as 297 to 198, nearly. A peculiarity of this pyramid is, that base is to altitude as apothem is to half base, Thus, 40 : 25 : : 32 : 20; that is, half base is a fourth proportional to base, apothem, and altitude.

§ 5. THE EXACT DIMENSIONS OF THE PYRAMIDS.

Figures 15 to 20 inclusive, show the linear dimensions

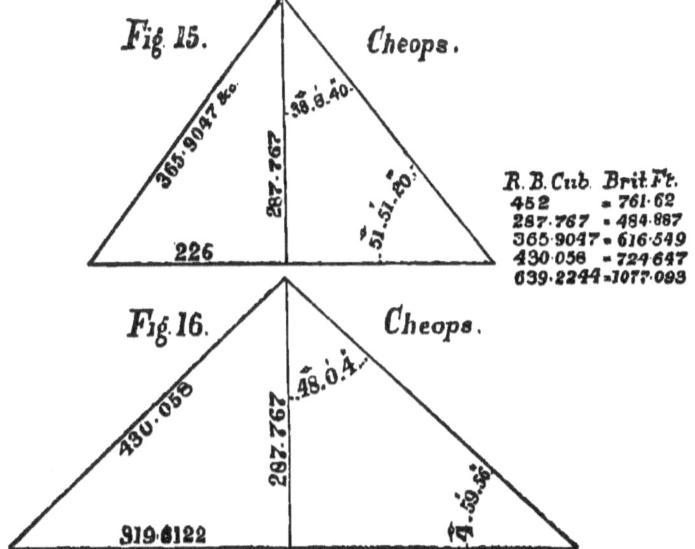

of the three pyramids, also their angles. The base angles are, Cheops, 51° 51′ 20″; Cephren, 52° 41′ 41″; and Mycerinus, 51° 19′ 4″.

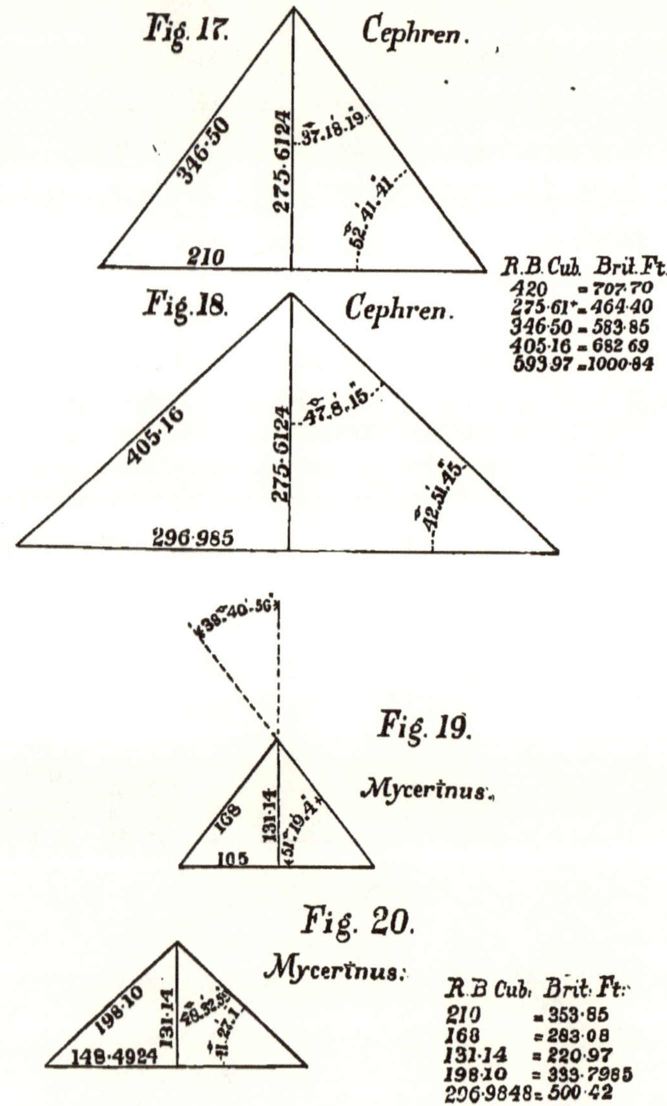

In Cheops, my dimensions agree with Piazzi Smyth—in the base of Cephren, with Vyse and Perring—in the height of Cephren, with Sir Gardner Wilkinson, nearly—in the base of Mycerinus, they agree with the usually accepted measures, and in the height of Mycerinus, they exceed Jas. J. Wild's measure, by not quite one of my cubits.

In my angles I agree very nearly with Piazzi Smyth, for Cheops, and with Agnew, for Cephren, differing about half a degree from Agnew, for Mycerinus, who took this pyramid to represent the same relation of π that P. Smyth ascribes to Cheops (viz.: $51° 51' 14''.3$), while he gave Cheops about the same angle which I ascribe to Mycerinus.

I shall now show how I make Cephren and Cheops of equal bases of 420 R.B. cubits at the same level, viz.—that of Cephren's base.

John James Wild made the bases of Cheops, Cephren, and Mycerinus, respectively, 80, 100, and 104·90 cubits above some point that he called Nile Level.

His cubit was, I believe, the Memphis, or Nilometric cubit—but at any rate, he made the base of Cephren 412 of them.

I therefore divided the recognized base of Cephren—viz., 707·75 British feet—by 412, and got a result of 1·7178 British feet for his cubit. Therefore, his measures multiplied by 1·7178 and divided by 1·685 will turn his cubits into R.B. cubits.

I thus make Cheops, Cephren, and Mycerinus, respectively, 81·56, 101·93, and 106·93 R.B. cubits above the datum that J. J. Wild calls Nile Level. According to Bonwick's "Facts and Fancies," p. 31, high water Nile would be 138½ ft. below base of Cheops (or 82.19 R.B. cubits).

Piazzi Smyth makes the pavement of Cheops 1752 British inches (or 86·64 R.B. cubits) above *average Nile Level*, but, by scaling his map, his *high Nile Level* appears to agree nearly with Wild.

It is the *relative levels* of the Pyramids, however, that I require, no matter how much above Nile Level.

Cephren's base of 420 cubits being 101·93 cubits, and Cheops' base of 452 cubits being 81·56 cubits above Wild's datum, the difference in level of their bases is, 20·37 cubits.

The ratio of base to altitude of Cheops being 330 to 210, therefore 20·37 cubits divided by 210 and multiplied by 330 equals 32 cubits; and 452 cubits minus 32 cubits, equals 420.

Similarly, the base of Mycerinus is 5 cubits *above* the base of Cephren, and the ratio of base to altitude 32 to 20; therefore, 5 cubits divided by 20 and multiplied by 32 equals 8 cubits to be *added* to the 210 cubit base of Mycerinus, making it 218 cubits in breadth at the level of Cephren's base.

Thus, a horizontal section or plan at the level of Cephren's base would meet the slopes of the Pyramids so that they would on plan appear as squares with sides

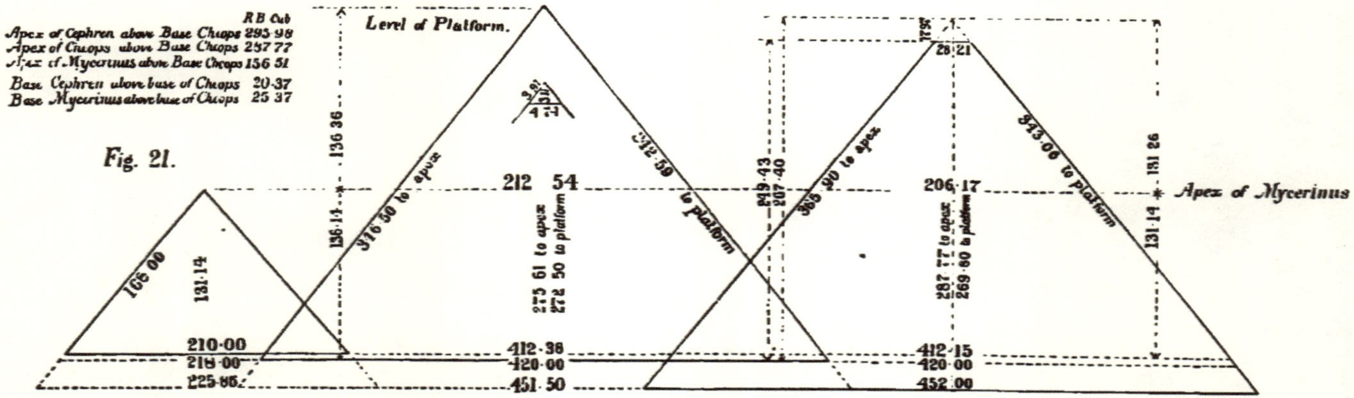

Fig. 21.

All the above dimensions are in R.B. cubits.

equal to 218, 420, and 420 R.B. cubits, for Mycerinus, Cephren, and Cheops, respectively.

Piazzi Smyth makes the top of the tenth course of Cheops 414 pyramid inches above the pavement; and 414 divided by 20·2006 equals 20·49 R.B. cubits.

But I have already proved that Cheops' 420 cubit base measure occurs at a level of 20·37 cubits above pavement; therefore is this level the level of the top of the tenth course, for the difference is only 0·12 R.B. cubits, or 2½ inches.

I wish here to note as a matter of interest, but not as affecting my theory, the following measures of Piazzi Smyth, turned into R.B. cubits, viz. :—

	PYR. INCHES.		R.B. CUBITS.
King's Chamber floor, above pavement..	1702·	=	84·25
Cheops' Base, as before stated........	9131·05	=	452·01
King's Chamber, "True Length,".. ...	412·132	=	20·40
" " "True First Height,".	230·389	=	11·40
" " "True Breadth,".....	206·066	=	10·20

He makes the present summit platform of Cheops 5445 pyramid inches above pavement. My calculation of 269·80 R.B. cub. (See Fig. 21) is equal to 5450 pyramid inches—this is about 18 cubits below the theoretical apex.

Figure 21 represents the comparative levels and dimensions of Mycerinus, Cephren, and Cheops.

The following peculiarities are noticeable:—That Cheops and Cephren are of equal bases at the level of Cephren's base;—that, at the level of Cheops' base, the latter is only half a cubit larger;—that, from the level of Mycerinus' base, Cheops is just double the height of Mycerinus;—and that from the level of Cephren's base, Cephren is just double the height of Mycerinus; measuring in the latter case, however, only up to the level platform at the summit of Cephren, which is said to be about eight feet wide.

The present summit of Cephren is 23·07 cubits above the present summit of Cheops, and the completed apex of Cephren would be 8·21 cubits above the completed apex of Cheops.

In the summit platforms I have been guided by P. Smyth's estimate of *height deficient*, 363 pyr. inches, for Cheops, and I have taken 8 feet base for Cephren's summit platform.

§ 6. GEOMETRICAL PECULIARITIES OF THE PYRAMIDS.

In any pyramid, the apothem is to half the base as the area of the four sides is to the area of the base.

Thus—Ratio apothem to half base Mycerinus. 32 to 20
" " " " Cephren .... 33 to 20
" " " " Cheops .... 34 to 21

	AREA OF THE FOUR SIDES.	AREA OF THE BASE.
Mycerinus	70560·	44100
Cephren	291060·	176400
Cheops	330777·90	204304

All in R.B. cubits.

Therefore—32	:	20	: :	70560·	:	44100
33	:	20	: :	291060·	:	176400
34	:	21	: :	330777·90	:	204304

* Herodotus states that "*the area of each of the four faces of Cheops was equal to the area of a square whose base was the altitude of a Pyramid;*" or, in other words, that altitude was a mean proportional to apothem and half base; thus—area of one face equals the fourth of 330777·90 or 82694·475 R.B. cubits, and the square root of 82694·475 is 287·56. But the correct altitude is 287·77, so the error is 0·21, or 4¼ British inches. I have therefore the authority of Herodotus to support the theory which I shall subsequently set forth, that this pyramid was the exponent of lines divided in mean and extreme ratio.

By taking the dimensions of the Pyramid from what I may call its *working level*, that is, the level of the base of Cephren, this peculiarity shows more clearly, as also others to which I shall refer. Thus—base of Cheops at working level, 420 cubits, and apothem 340 cubits; base area is, therefore, 176400 cubits, and area of one face is (420 cubits, multiplied by half apothem, or 170 cubits) 71400 cubits. Now the square root of 71400 would give altitude, or side of square equal to altitude, 267·207784 cubits: but the real altitude is $\sqrt{340^2 - 210^2} = \sqrt{71500} = 267{\cdot}394839$. So that the error of Herodotus's proposition is the difference between $\sqrt{714}$ and $\sqrt{715}$.

* Proctor is responsible for this statement, as I am quoting from an essay of his in the *Gentleman's Magazine*. R. B.

This leads to a consideration of the properties of the angle formed by the ratio *apothem* 34 to *half base* 21, peculiar to the pyramid Cheops. (*See Figure* 22.)

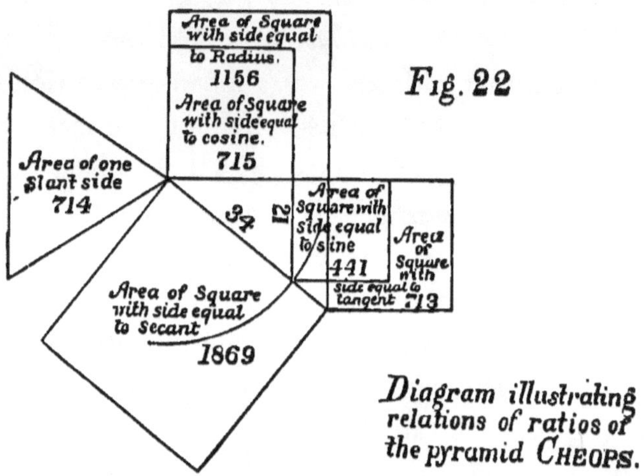

Fig. 22

Diagram illustrating relations of ratios of the pyramid CHEOPS.

Calling apothem 34, *radius;* and half base 21, *sine* —I find that—

Radius is the square root of	1156
Sine....................	441
Co-sine....................	715
Tangent....................	713
Secant....................	1869
and Co-versed-sine.............	169

So it follows that the area of one of the faces, 714, is a mean between the square of the altitude or co-sine, 715, and the square of the tangent, 713.

Thus the reader will notice that the peculiarities of

the Pyramid Cheops lie in the regular relations of the *squares* of its various lines; while the peculiarities of the other two pyramids lie in the relations of the lines themselves.

Mycerinus and Cephren, born, as one may say, of those two noble triangles 3, 4, 5, and 20, 21, 29, exhibit in their lineal developments ratios so nearly perfect that, for all practical purposes, they may be called correct.

Thus—Mycerinus, (a) $20^2 + 25^2 = 1025$, and $32^2 = 1024$.
and Cephren, (b) $80^2 + 105^2 = 17425$, and $132^2 = 17424$.
or (c) $400^2 + 431^2 = 345761$, and $588^2 = 345744$.

See diagrams, Figures 11 to 14 inclusive.

In the Pyramid Cheops, altitude is *very nearly* a mean proportional between apothem and half base. Apothem being 34, and half base 21, then altitude would be $\sqrt{34^2 - 21^2} = \sqrt{715} = 26{\cdot}7394839$, and—

21 : 26·7394839 : : 26·7394839 : 34, nearly.

Here, of course, the same difference comes in as occurred in considering the assumption of Herodotus, viz., the difference between $\sqrt{715}$ and $\sqrt{714}$; because if the altitude were $\sqrt{714}$, then would it be *exactly* a mean proportional between the half base and the apothem; (thus, 21 : 26·72077 : : 26·72077 : : 34.)

(a) Half base to altitude. (b) Half base to altitude. (c) Half diagonal of base to altitude.

In Cheops, the ratios of apothem, half base and edge are, 34, 21, and 40, very nearly, thus, $34^2 \times 21^2 =$ 1597, and $40^2 = 1600$.

The dimensions of Cheops (from the level of the base of Cephren) to be what Piazzi Smyth calls a π pyramid, would be—

Half base	210	R.B. cubits.
Altitude	267·380304, &c.	"
Apothem	339·988573, &c.	"

Altitude being to perimeter of base, as radius of a circle to circumference.

My dimensions of the pyramid therefore in which—

Half base	= 210	R.B. cubits.
Altitude	= 267·394839 &c.	"
Apothem	= 340	"

come about as near to the ratio of π as it is possible to come, and provide simple lines and templates to the workmen in constructing the building; and I entertain no doubt that on the simple lines and templates that my ratios provide, were these three pyramids built.

§ 6A THE CASING STONES OF THE PYRAMIDS.

Figures 23, 24, and 25, represent ordinary casing stones of the three pyramids, and Figures 26, 27, and 28, represent angle or quoin casing stones of the same.

The casing stone of Cheops, found by Colonel Vyse, is represented in Bonwick's "Pyramid Facts and Fancies," page 16, as measuring four feet three inches at the top, eight feet three inches at the bottom, four feet

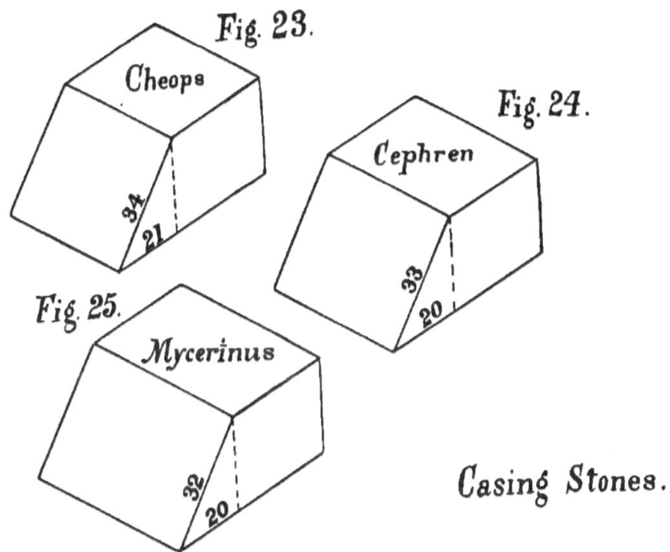

Casing Stones.

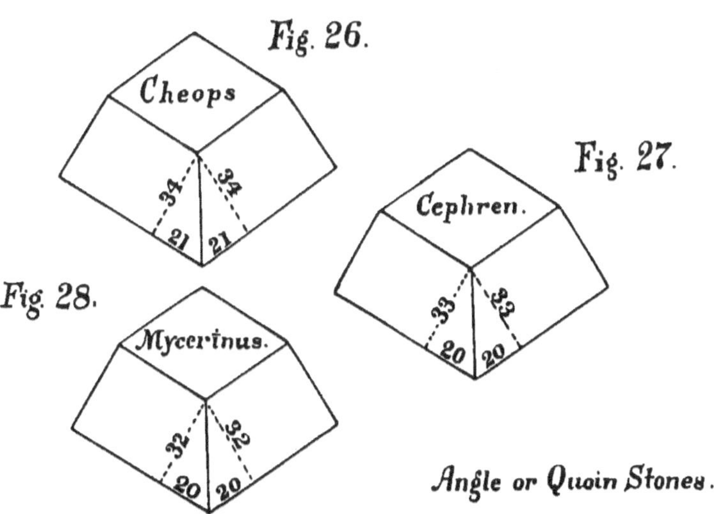

Angle or Quoin Stones.

LIBRARY
OF THE
UNIVERSITY
CALIFORNIA.

eleven inches at the back, and six feet three inches at the front. Taking four feet eleven inches as *Radius*, and six feet three inches as *Secant*, then the *Tangent* is three feet ten inches and three tenths.

Thus, in inches $(\sqrt{75^2 - 59^2}) = 46{\cdot}30$ inches; therefore the inclination of the stone must have been—slant height 75 inches to 46·30 inches horizontal. Now, 46·30 is to 75, as 21 is to 34. Therefore, Col. Vyse's casing stone agrees exactly with my ratio for the Pyramid Cheops, viz., 21 to 34. (*See Figure* 29.)

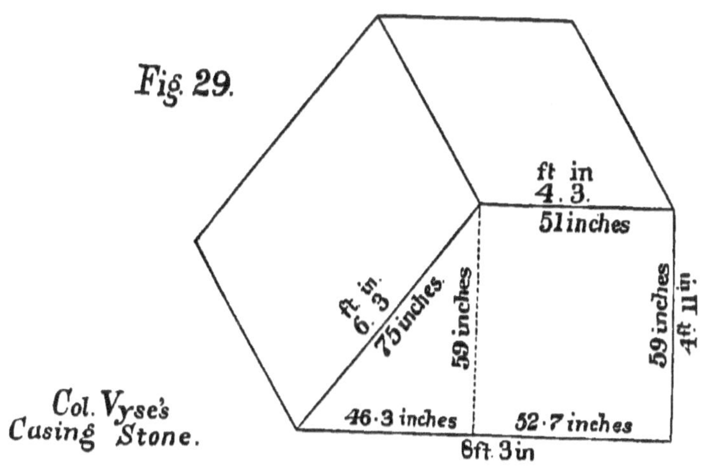

This stone must have been out of plumb at the back an inch and seven tenths; perhaps to give room for grouting the back joint of the marble casing stone to the limestone body of the work: or, because, as it is not a necessity in good masonry that the back of a stone should be exactly plumb, so long as the error is on the right side, the builders might not have been particular in that respect.

Figure 59 represents such a template as the masons

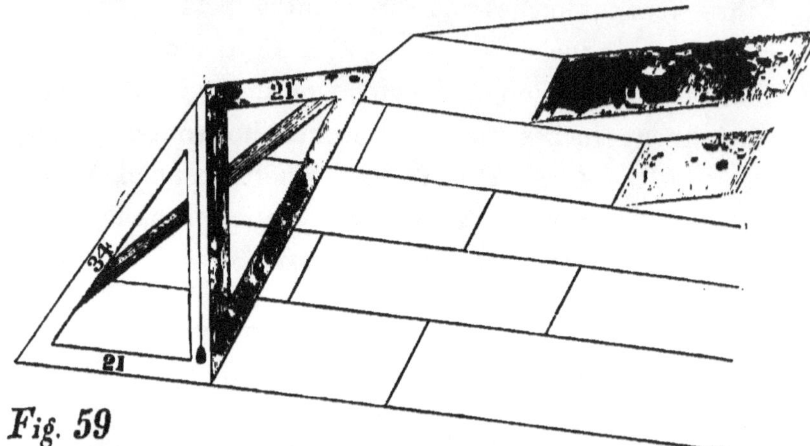

Fig. 59
(Templet of Cheops. standing at angle of wall.)

would have used in building Cheops, both for dressing and setting the stones. (The courses are drawn out of proportion to the template.) The other pyramids must have been built by the aid of similar templates.

Such large blocks of stone as were used in the casing of these pyramids could not have been completely dressed before setting; the back and ends, and the top and bottom beds were probably dressed off truly, and the face roughly scabbled off; but the true slope angle could not have been dressed off until the stone had been truly set and bedded, otherwise there would have been great danger to the sharp arrises.

I shall now record the peculiarities of the 3, 4, 5 or

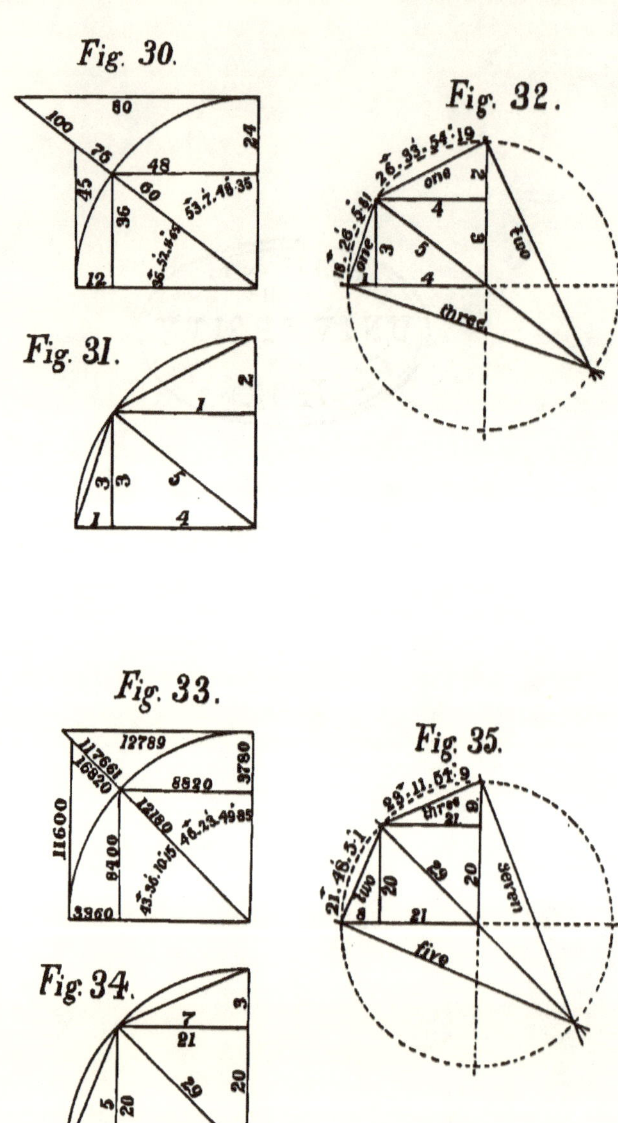
Fig. 30.
80
100
75
24
48
45
60
36
12
Fig. 31.
2
1
3
3
5
1
4
Fig. 32.
one
4
3
5
6
one
4
two
three
Fig. 33.
12789
3780
8820
11600
12180
8400
3360
Fig. 34.
7
3
21
5
20
29
20
2
21
Fig. 35.
three
21
20
29
20
a two
21
seven
five

Pythagorean triangle, and the right-angled triangle 20, 21, 29.

§ 7. PECULIARITIES OF THE TRIANGLES 3, 4, 5, AND 20, 21, 29.

The 3, 4, 5 triangle contains 36° 52′ 11·65″ and the complement or greater angle 53° 7′ 48·35″

Radius........5	=	60	whole numbers.*
Co-sine........4	=	48	"
Sine...........3	=	36	"
Versed sine ... 1	=	12	"
Co-versed sine 2	=	24	"
Tangent 3¾	=	45	"
Secant........6¼	=	75	"
Co-tangent....6⅔	=	80	"
Co-secant.....8⅓	=	100	"

Tangent + Secant = Diameter or 2 Radius
Co tan. + Co-sec = 3 Radius
Sine : Versed-sine :: 3 : 1
Co-sine : Co-versed sine :: 2 : 1

Figure 30 illustrates the preceding description. Figure 31 shows the 3·1 triangle, and the 2·1 triangle built up on the sine and co-sine of the 3, 4, 5 triangle.

The 3·1 triangle contains 18° 26′ 5·82″ and the 2·1 triangle 26° 33′ 54·19″; the latter has been frequently noticed as a pyramid angle in the gallery inclinations.

Figure 32 shows these two triangles combined with the 3, 4, 5 triangle, on the circumference of a circle.

---

* 60 = 3 × 4 × 5

The 20, 21, 29 triangle contains 43° 36′ 10·15″ and the complement, 46° 23′ 49·85″.

Expressed in whole numbers—

Radius.......	29	=	12180*
Sine..........	20	=	8400
Co-sine	21	=	8820
Versed sine...	8	=	3360
Co-versed sine	9	=	3780
Tangent.....		=	11600
Co-tangent....		=	12789
Secant.......		=	16820
Co-sec........		=	17661

Tangent + Secant = 2⅓ radius

Co-tan. + Co-sec = 2½ radius

Sine : Versed sine :: 5 : 2

Co-sine : Co-versed sine :: 7 : 3

It is noticeable that while the multiplier required to bring radius 5 and the rest into whole numbers, for the 3, 4, 5 triangle is twelve, in the 20, 21, 29 triangle it is 420, the key measure for the bases of the two main pyramids in R.B. cubits.†

I am led to believe from study of the plan, and consideration of the whole numbers in this 20, 21, 29 triangle, that the R.B. cubit, like the Memphis cubit, was divided into 280 parts.

The whole numbers of radius, sine, and co-sine divided by 280, give a very pretty measure and series in R.B. cubits, viz., 43½, 30, and 31½, or 87, 60, and 63, or 174, 120

* 12180 = 20 × 21 × 29

† 12 = 3 × 4, and 420 = 20 × 21

and 126;—all exceedingly useful in right-angled measurements. Notice that the right-angled triangle 174, 120, 126, in the sum of its sides *amounts to* 420.

Figure 33 illustrates the 20, 21, 29 triangle. Figure 34 shows the 5·2 and 7·3 triangles built up on the sine and co-sine of the 20, 21, 29 triangle.

The 5·2 triangle contains 21° 48′ 5·08″ and the 7·3 triangle 23° 11′ 54·98″.

Figure 35 shows how these two triangles are combined with the 20, 21, 29 triangle on the circumference, and Figure 36 gives a general view and identification of

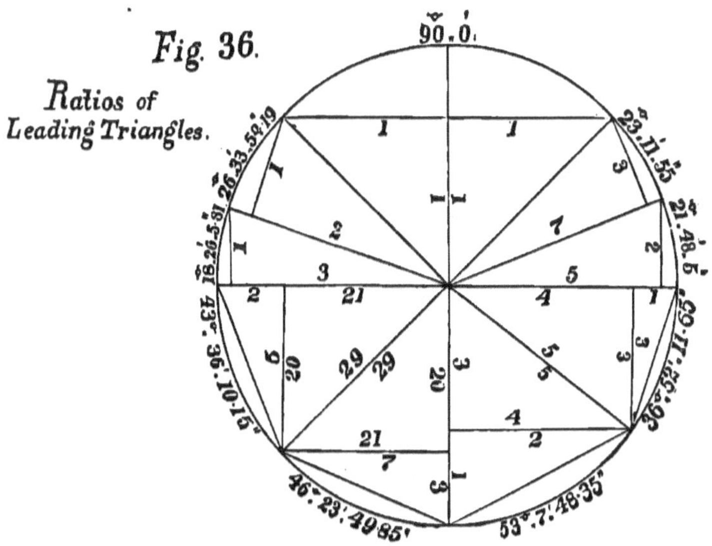

Fig. 36.
Ratios of Leading Triangles.

these six triangles which occupied an important position in the trigonometry of a people who did all their work by right angles and proportional lines.

§ 8. GENERAL OBSERVATIONS.

It must be admitted that in the details of the building of the Pyramids of Gïzeh there are traces of other measures than R.B. cubits, but that the original cubit of the plan was 1·685 British feet I feel no doubt. It is a perfect and beautiful measure, fit for such a noble design, and, representing as it does the sixtieth part of a second of the Earth's polar circumference, it is and was a measure for all time.

It may be objected that these ancient geometricians could not have been aware of the measure of the Earth's circumference; and wisely so, were it not for two distinct answers that arise. The first being, that since I think I have shown that Pythagoras never discovered the Pythagorean triangle, but that it must have been known and practically employed thousands of years before his era, in the Egyptian Colleges where he obtained his M.A. degree, so in the same way it is probable that Eratosthenes, when he went to work to prove that the earth's circumference was fifty times the distance from Syene to Alexandria, may have obtained the idea from his ready access to the ill-fated Alexandrian Library, in which perhaps some record of the learning of the builders of the Pyramids was stored. And therefore I claim that there is no reason why the pyramid builders should not have known as much about the circumference of the earth as the modern world that has calmly stood by in its ignorance and permitted those magnificent and, as I shall prove, useful edifices to be stripped of their beautiful garments of polished marble.

My second answer is that the correct cubit measure may have been got by its inventors in a variety of other ways; for instance, by observations of shadows of heavenly bodies, without any knowledge even that the earth was round; or it may have been evolved like the British inch, which Sir John Herschel tells us is within a thousandth part of being one five hundred millionth of the earth's polar axis. I doubt if the circumference of the earth was considered by the inventor of the British inch.

It was a peculiarity of the Hindoo mathematicians that they tried to make out that all they knew was *very old.* Modern savants appear to take the opposite stand for any little information they happen to possess.

The cubit which is called the Royal Babylonian cubit and stated to measure 0·5131 metre, differs so slightly from my cubit, only the six-hundredth part of a foot, that it may fairly be said to be the same cubit, and it will be for antiquaries to trace the connection, as this may throw some light on the identity of the builders of the Pyramids of Gïzeh. Few good English two-foot rules agree better than these two cubits do.

While I was groping about in the dark searching for this bright needle, I tried on the plan many likely ancient measures.

For a long time I worked in Memphis or Nilometric

cubits, which I made 1·7126 British feet; they seem to vary from 1·70 to 1·72, and although I made good use of them in identifying other people's measures, still they were evidently not in accordance with the design; but the R.B. cubit of 1·685 British feet works as truly into the plan of the Pyramids *without fractions* as it does into the circumference of the earth.

Here I might, to prevent others from falling into one of my errors, point out a rock on which I was aground for a long time. I took the base of the Pyramid Cheops, determined by Piazzi Smyth, from Bonwick's "Pyramid Facts and Fancies" (a valuable little reference book), as 763.81 British feet, and the altitude as 486.2567; and then from Piazzi Smyth's "Inheritance," page 27, I confirmed these figures, and so worked on them for a long time, but found always a great flaw in my work, and at last adopted a fresh base for Cheops, feeling sure that Mr. Smyth's base was wrong: for I was absolutely grounded in my conviction that at a certain level, Cheops' and Cephren's measures bore certain relations to each other. I subsequently found in another part of Mr. Smyth's book, that the correct measures were 761.65 and 484.91 British feet for base and altitude, which were exactly what I wanted, and enabled me to be in accordance with him in that pyramid which he appears to have made his particular study.

For the information of those who may wish to compare my measures, which are the results of an even or regular circumference without fractions, with Mr. Smyth's measures, which are the results of an even or regular diameter without fractions, it may be well to state that there are just about 99 R.B. cubits in 80 of Piazzi Smyth's cubits of·25 pyramid inches each.

§ 9. THE PYRAMIDS OF EGYPT, THE THEODOLITES OF THE EGYPTIAN LAND SURVEYORS.

About twenty-three years ago, on my road to Australia, I was crossing from Alexandria to Cairo, and saw the pyramids of Gïzeh.

I watched them carefully as the train passed along, noticed their clear cut lines against the sky, and their constantly changing relative position.

I then felt a strong conviction that they were built for at least one useful purpose, and that purpose was the survey of the country. I said, "Here be the Theodolites of the Egyptians."

Built by scientific men, well versed in geometry, but unacquainted with the use of glass lenses, these great stone monuments are so suited in shape for the purposes of land surveying, that the practical engineer or surveyor must, after consideration, admit that they may have been built mainly for that purpose.

Not only might the country have been surveyed by these great instruments, and the land allotted at periodical times to the people; but they, remaining always in one position, were there to correct and readjust boundaries destroyed or confused by the annual inundations of the Nile.

The Pyramids of Egypt may be considered as a great system of landmarks for the establishment and easy readjustment at any time of the boundaries of the holdings of the people.

The Pyramids of Gïzeh appear to have been main marks; and those of Abousir, Sakkârah, Dashow, Lisht, Meydoun, &c., with the great pyramids in Lake Mœris, subordinate marks, in this system, which was probably extended from Chaldæa through Egypt into Ethiopia.

The pyramid builders may perhaps have made the entombment of their Kings one of their exoteric objects, playing on the morbid vanity of their rulers to induce them to the work, but in the minds of the builders before ever they built must have been planted the intention to make use of the structures for the purposes of land surveying.

The land of Egypt was valuable and maintained a dense population; every year it was mostly submerged, and the boundaries destroyed or confused. Every soldier had six to twelve acres of land; the priests had their slice of the land too; after every war a reallotment of the lands must have taken place, perhaps every year.

While the water was lying on the land, it so softened the ground that the stone boundary marks must have required frequent readjustment, as they would have been likely to fall on one side.

By the aid of their great stone theodolites, the surveyors, who belonged to the priestly order, were able to readjust the boundaries with great precision. That all science was comprised in their secret mysteries may be one reason why no hieroglyphic record of the scientific uses of the pyramids remains. It is possible that at the time of Diodorus and Herodotus, (and even when Pythagoras visited Egypt,) theology may have so smothered science, that the uses of the pyramids may have been forgotten by the very priests to whom in former times the knowledge belonged; but "a respectful reticence" which has been noticed in some of these old writers on pyramid and other priestly matters would rather lead us to believe that an initiation into the mysteries may have sealed their lips on subjects about which they might otherwise have been more explicit.

The "*closing*" of one pyramid over another in bringing any of their many lines into true order, must even now be very perfect;—but now we can only imagine the beauties of these great instrumental wonders of the world when the casing stones were on them. We can picture the rosy lights of one, and the bright white lights of others; their clear cut lines against the sky, true as the hairs of a theodolite; and the sombre darkness of the contrasting shades, bringing out their angles with startling distinctness. Under the influence of the Eastern sun, the faces must have been a very blaze of light, and could have been seen at enormous distances like great mirrors.

I declare that the pyramids of Gïzeh in all their

polished glory, before the destroyer stripped them of their beautiful garments, were in every respect adapted to flash around clearly defined lines of sight, upon which the lands of the nation could be accurately threaded. The very thought of these mighty theodolites of the old Egyptians fills me with wonder and reverence. What perfect and beautiful instruments they were! never out of adjustment, always correct, always ready; no magnetic deviation to allow for. No wonder they took the trouble they did to build them so correctly in their so marvellously suitable positions.

If Astronomers agree that observations of a pole star could have been accurately made by peering up a small gallery on the north side of one of the pyramids only a few hundred feet in length, I feel that I shall have little difficulty in satisfying them that accurate measurements to points only *miles* away could have been made from angular observations of the whole group.

§ 10. HOW THE PYRAMIDS WERE MADE USE OF.

It appears from what I have already set forth that the plan of the Pyramids under consideration is geometrically exact, a perfect set of measures.

I shall now show how these edifices were applied to a thoroughly geometrical purpose in the true meaning of the word—to measure the Earth.

I shall show how true straight lines could be extended from the Pyramids in given directions useful in right-angled trigonometry, by direct observation of the buildings, and without the aid of other instruments.

And I shall show how by the aid of a simple instrument angles could be exactly observed from any point.

This Survey theory does not stand or fall on the merits of my theory of the Gïzeh plan. Let it be proved that this group is not built on the exact system of triangulation set forth by me, it is still a fact that its plan is in a similar shape, and any such shape would enable a surveyor acquainted with the plan to lay down accurate surveys by observations of the group even should it not occupy the precise lines assumed by me.

And here I must state that although the lines of the plan as laid down herein agree nearly with the lines as laid down in Piazzi Smyth's book, in the Penny Cyclopædia, and in an essay of Proctor's in the *Gentleman's Magazine*, still I find that they do not agree at all satisfactorily with a map of the Pyramids in Sharp's "Egypt," said to be copied from Wilkinson's map.

We will, however, for the time, and to explain my survey theory, suppose the plan theory to be correct, as I firmly believe it is.

And then, supposing it may be proved that the respective positions of the pyramids are slightly different to those that I have allotted to them on my plan, it will only make a similar slight difference to the lines and angles which I shall here show could be laid out by their aid.

Let us in the first place comprehend clearly the shape of the land of Egypt.

A sector or fan, with a long handle—the fan or sector, the delta; and the handle of the fan, the Nile Valley, running nearly due south.

The Pyramids of Gïzeh are situate at the angle of the sector, on a rocky eminence whence they can all be seen for many miles. The summits of the two high ones can be seen from the delta, and from the Nile Valley to a very great distance; how far, I am unable to say; but I should think that while the group could be made general use of for a radius of fifteen miles, the summits of Cephren and Cheops could be made use of for a distance of thirty miles; taking into consideration the general fall of the country.

It must be admitted that if meridian observations of the star Alpha of the Dragon could be made with accuracy by peeping up a small hole in one of the pyramids, then surely might the surveyors have carried true north and south lines up the Nile Valley as far as the summit of Cheops was visible, by "*plumbing in*" the star and the apex of the pyramid by the aid of a string and a stone.

True east and west lines could have been made to intersect such north and south lines from the various groups of pyramids along the river banks, by whose aid also such lines would be prolonged.

Next, supposing that their astronomers had been aware of the latitude of Cheops, and the annual northing and southing of the sun, straight lines could have been laid out in various sectoral directions to the north-eastward and north-westward of Cheops, across the delta, as far as the extreme apex of the pyramid was visible, by observations of the sun, rising or setting over his summit. (That the Dog-star was observed in this manner from the north-west, I have little doubt.)

For this purpose, surveyors would be stationed at suitable distances apart with their strings and their stones, ready to catch the sun simultaneously, and at the very moment he became transfixed upon the apex of the pyramid, and was, as it were, "swallowed by it." (*See Figure* 37.) The knowledge of the pyramid slope

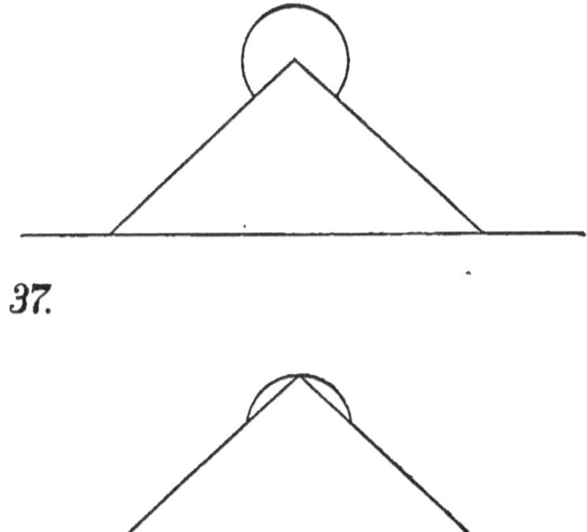

Fig. 37.

angle from different points of view would enable the

surveyor to place himself in readiness nearly on the line.

Surely such lines as these would be as true and as perfect as we could lay out nowadays with all our modern instrumental appliances. A string and a stone here, a clean-cut point of stone twenty miles away, and a great ball of fire behind that point at a distance of ninety odd million miles. The error in such a line would be very trifling.

Such observations as last mentioned would have been probably extended from Cephren for long lines, as being the higher pyramid above the earth's surface, and may have been made from the moon or stars.

In those days was the sun the intimate friend of man. The moon and stars were his hand-maidens.

How many of us can point to the spot of the sun's rising or setting? We, with our clocks, and our watches, and our compasses, rarely observe the sun or stars. But in a land and an age when the sun was the only clock, and the pyramid the only compass, the movements and positions of the heavenly bodies were known to all. These people were *familiar* with the stars, and kept a watch upon their movements.

How many of our vaunted educated population could point out the Dog-star in the heavens?—but the whole Egyptian nation hailed his rising as the beginning of their year, and as the harbinger of their annual blessing, the rising of the waters of the Nile.

It is possible therefore that the land surveyors of

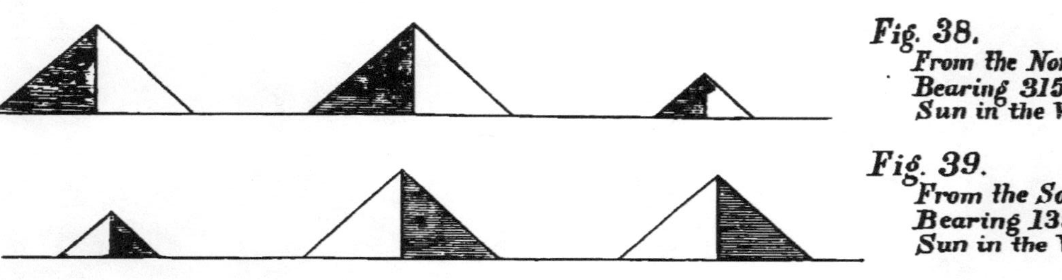

Fig. 38.
From the North West
Bearing 315°
Sun in the West.

Fig. 39.
From the South East
Bearing 135°
Sun in the West.

Fig. 40.
From the North East
Bearing 45°
Sun in the East.

Fig. 41.
From the South West
Bearing 225°
Sun in the East.

Egypt made full use of the heavenly bodies in their surveys of the land; and while we are pitifully laying out our new countries by the circumferenter and the compass, we presume to speak slightingly of the supposed dark heathen days, when the land of Egypt was surveyed by means of the sun and the stars, and the theodilites were built of stone, with vertical limbs five hundred feet in height, and horizontal limbs three thousand feet in diameter.

Imagine half a dozen such instruments as this in a distance of about sixty miles (for each group of pyramids was effectually such an instrument), and we can form some conception of the perfection of the surveys of an almost prehistoric nation.

The centre of Lake Mœris, in which Herodotus tells us two pyramids stood 300 feet above the level of the lake, appears from the maps to be about S. 28° W., or S. 29° W. from Gïzeh, distant about 57 miles, and the Meidân group of pyramids appears to be about 33 miles due south of Gïzeh.

Figures 38, 39, 40 and 41, show that north-west, south-east, north-east, and south-west lines from the pyramids could be extended by simply plumbing the angles. These lines would be run in sets of two's and three's, according to the number of pyramids in the group; and their known distances apart at that angle would check the correctness of the work.

A splendid line was the line bearing 43° 36′ 10·15″, or 223° 36′ 10·15″ from Cheops and Cephren, the pyramids covering each other, the line of hypotenuse of the great 20, 21, 29 triangle of the plan. This I call the 20, 21 line. (*See Figure* 42.)

Figure 43 represents the 3, 4, 5 triangle line from the summits of Mycerinus and Cheops in true line bearing 216° 52′ 11·65″. This I call the south 4, west 3 line.

The next line is what I call the 2, 1 line, and is illustrated by figure 44. It is one of the most perfect of the series, and bears S. 26° 33′ 54·19″ W. from the apex of Cephren. This line demonstrates clearly why Mycerinus was cased with red granite.

Not in memory of the beautiful and rosy-cheeked Nitocris, as some of the tomb theory people say, but for a less romantic but more useful object; simply because, from this quarter, and round about, the lines of the pyramids would have been confused if Mycerinus had not been of a different color. The 2, 1 line is a line in which Mycerinus would have been absolutely lost in the slopes of Cephren but for his red color. There is not a fact that more clearly establishes my theory, and the wisdom and forethought of those who planned the Gïzeh pyramids, than this red pyramid Mycerinus, and the 2, 1 line.

Hekeyan Bey, speaks of this pyramid as of a "*ruddy complexion;*" John Greaves quotes from the Arabic book, Morat Alzeman, "*and the lesser which is coloured;*" and an Arabic writer who dates the Pyramids three hundred years before the Flood, and cannot find among the learned men of Egypt "*any certain relation*

Fig. 42.
South 21. West 20.
Bearing 223°. 36'. 10·15".

Fig. 43
South 4. West 3.
Bearing 216°. 52'. 11·65".

Fig. 44.
South 2. West 1.
Bearing 206°. 33'. 54·18".

Fig. 45.
South 96. West 55.
Bearing 209°. 48'. 32·81".

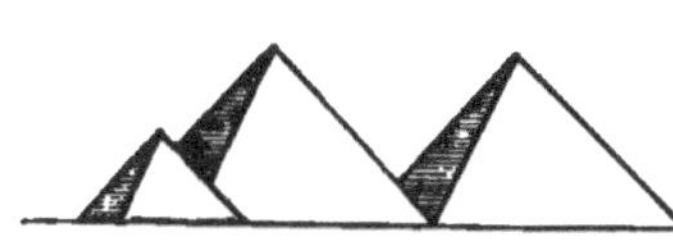

Fig. 46.
South 3, West 1.
Bearing 198°. 26'. 5·82"

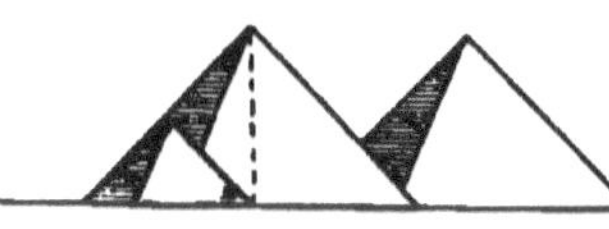

Fig. 47.
South 5, West 2.
Bearing 201°. 48'. 5".

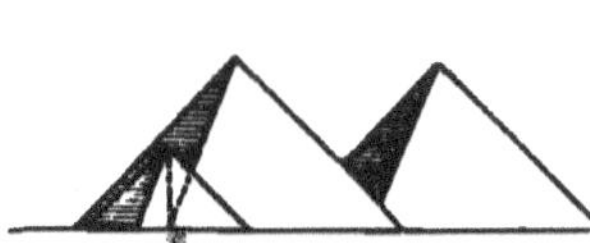

Fig. 48.
South 7. West 3.
Bearing 203°. 11'. 55".

concerning them," nor any "*memory of them amongst men,*" also expatiates upon the beauties of the "*coloured satin*" covering of this one particular pyramid.

Figure 45 represents the line south 96, west 55, from Cephren, bearing 209° 48′ 32·81″; the apex of Cephren is immediately above the apex of Mycerinus.

Figure 46 is the S. 3 W. 1 line, bearing 198° 26′ 5.82″; here the dark slope angle of the pyramids with the sun to the eastward occupies half of the apparent half base.

Figure 47 is the S. 5, W. 2 line, bearing 201° 48′ 5″; here Cephren and Mycerinus are in outside slope line.

Figure 48 is the S. 7 W. 3 line, bearing 203° 11′ 55″; here the inside slope of Cephren springs from the centre of the apparent base of Mycerinus.

I must content myself with the preceding examples of a few pyramid lines, but must have said enough to show that from every point of the compass their appearance was distinctly marked and definitely to be determined by surveyors acquainted with the plan.

§ 11. DESCRIPTION OF THE ANCIENT PORTABLE SURVEY INSTRUMENT.

I must now commence with a single pyramid, show how approximate observations could be made from it, and then extend the theory to a group with the observations thereby rendered more perfect and delicate.

We will suppose the surveyor to be standing looking at the pyramid Cephren; he knows that its base is

420 cubits, and its apothem 346½ cubits. He has provided himself with a model in wood, or stone, or metal, and one thousandth of its size—therefore his model will be 0.42 cubit base, and 0.3465 cubit apothem—or, in round numbers, eight and half inches base, and seven inches apothem.

This model is fixed on the centre of a card or disc, graduated from the centre to the circumference, like a compass card, to the various points of the compass, or divisions of a circle.

The model pyramid is fastened due north and south on the lines of this card or disc, so that when the north point of the card points north, the north face of the model pyramid faces to the north.

The surveyor also has a table, which, with a pair of plumb lines or mason's levels, he can erect quite level: this table is also graduated from the centre with divisions of a circle, or points of the compass, and it is larger than the card or disc attached to the model.

This table is made so that it can revolve upon its stand, and can be clamped. We will call it the *lower limb.* There is a pin in the centre of the lower limb, and a hole in the centre of the disc bearing the model, which can be thus placed upon the centre of the table, and becomes the *upper limb.* The upper limb can be clamped to the lower limb.

The first process will be to clamp both upper and lower limbs together, with the north and south lines of both in unison, then revolve both limbs on the stand till the north and south line points straight for the pyramid in the distance, which is done by the aid of sights erected at the north and south points of the perimeter of the lower limb. When this is adjusted, clamp the lower limb and release the upper limb; now revolve the upper limb until the model pyramid exactly covers the pyramid in the distance, and shows just the same shade on one side and light on the other, when viewed from the sights of the clamped lower limb—and the lines, angles, and shades of the model coincide with the lines, angles, and shades of the pyramid observed;—now clamp the upper limb. Now does the model stand really due north and south, the same as the pyramid in the distance; it throws the same shades, and exhibits the same angles when seen from the same point of view; just as much of it is in shade and as much of it is in light as the pyramid under observation; therefore it must be standing due north and south, because Cephren himself is standing due north and south, and the upper limb reads off on the lower limb the angle or bearing observed.

So far we possess an instrument equal to the modern circumferenter, and yet we have only brought one pyramid into work.

If I have shown that such an operation as the above is practically feasible, if I have shown that angles can be taken with moderate accuracy by observing one pyramid of 420 cubits base, how much more accurate will the observation be when the surveyor's plane table bears a group of pyramids which occupy a representative space of about 1400 cubits when viewed from the south or north, and about 1760 cubits when viewed from the east or west. If situated a mile or two south of the Gïzeh group our surveyor could also tie in and perfect his work by sights to the Sâkkarah group with Sâkkarah models; and so on, up the Nile Valley, he would find every few miles groups of pyramids by aid of which he would be enabled to tie his work together.

If the Gïzeh group of pyramids is placed and shaped in the manner I have described, it must be clear that an exact model and plan, say a thousandth of the size, could be very easily made—the plan being at the level of the base of Cephren where the bases of the two main pyramids are even;—and if they are not exactly so placed and shaped, it may be admitted that their position and dimensions were known to the surveyors or priests, so that such models could be constructed. It is probable, therefore, that the instrument used in conjunction with these pyramids, was a machine constructed in a similar manner to the simple machine I have described, only instead of there being but one model pyramid on the disc or upper limb, it bore the whole group; and the smaller pyramids were what we may call vernier points in this great circle, enabling the surveyor to mark off known angles with great accuracy by noticing how, as he worked round the group of pyramids, one or other of the smaller ones was covered by its neighbours.*

* See general plan of Gïzeh Group op. page 1.

The immensity of the main pyramids would require the smaller ones to be used for surveys in the immediate neighbourhood, as the surveyor might easily be too close to get accurate observations from the main pyramids.

The upper limb, then, was a disc or circular plate bearing the model of the group.

Cheops would be situated in the centre of the circle, and observations would be taken by bringing the whole model group into even line and even light and shade with the Gïzeh group.

I believe that with a reasonable-sized model occupying a circle of six or seven feet diameter, such as a couple of men could carry, very accurate bearings could have been taken, and probably were taken.

The pyramid shape is the very shape of all others to employ for such purposes. A cone would be useless, because the lights and shades would be softened off and its angles from all points would be the same. Other solids with perpendicular angles would be useless, because although they would vary in width from different points of view they would not present that ever changing angle that a pyramid does when viewed from different directions.

After familiarity with the models which I have made use of in prosecuting these investigations, I find that I can judge with great accuracy *from their appearance only* the bearing of the group from any point at which I stand. I make bold to say that the pocket compass of the Egyptian surveyor was a little model of the group of pyramids in his district, and he had only to hold it up on his hand and turn it round in the sun till its shades and angles corresponded with the appearance of the group, to tell as well as we could tell by our compasses, perhaps better, his bearing from the landmarks that governed his surveys.

The Great Circle of Gold described by Diodorus (*Diod. Sic. lib. X., part* 2, *cap.* 1) as having been employed by the Egyptians, and on which was marked amongst other things, the position of the rising and setting of the stars, and stated by him to have been carried off by Cambysses when Egypt was conquered by the Persians, is supposed by Cassini to have been also employed for finding the meridian by observation of the rising and setting of the sun. This instrument and others described by writers on Egypt would have been in practice very similar to the instrument which I have described as having been probably employed for terrestrial observations.

The table or disc comprising the lower limb of the instrument, might have been supported upon a small stand with a circular hole in the centre, so arranged that the instrument could be either set up alone and supported by its own tripod, or rested fairly on the top of any of those curious stone boundary marks which were made use of, not only to mark the corners of the different holdings, but to show the level of the Nile inundations. (*See Figure* 49, *copied from Sharpe's Egypt,*

vol. I., p. 6.) The peculiar shape of the top of these stone landmarks, or "sacred boundary stones," appears suitable for such purposes, and it would have been a great convenience to the surveyor, and conducive to accuracy, that it should be so arranged that the instrument should be fixed immediately over the mark, as appears probable from the shape of the stone.

A noticeable point in this theory is, that it is not in the least essential that the apex of a pyramid should be complete. If their summits were left permanently flat, they would work in for survey purposes quite as well, and I think better, than if carried to a point, and they would be more useful with a flat top for defined shadows when used as sun dials.

In the Gïzeh group, the summit of Cheops appears to me to have been left incomplete the better to get the range with Cephren for lines down the delta.

In this system of surveying, there is always a beautiful connection between the horizontal bearings and the apparent or observed angles presented by the slopes and edges of the pyramid. Thus, in pyramids like those of Gïzeh, which stand north and south, and whose meridional sections contain less, and whose diagonal sections contain more than a right angle, the vertex being the point at which the angle is measured—this law holds :—

That the smallest interior angle at the vertex, contained between the inside edge and the outside edge, will exhibit the same angle as the bearing of the observer's eye from the apex of the pyramid *when the angle at the apex contained by the outside edges appears to be a right angle.*

Figures 50 to 55 inclusive illustrate this beautiful

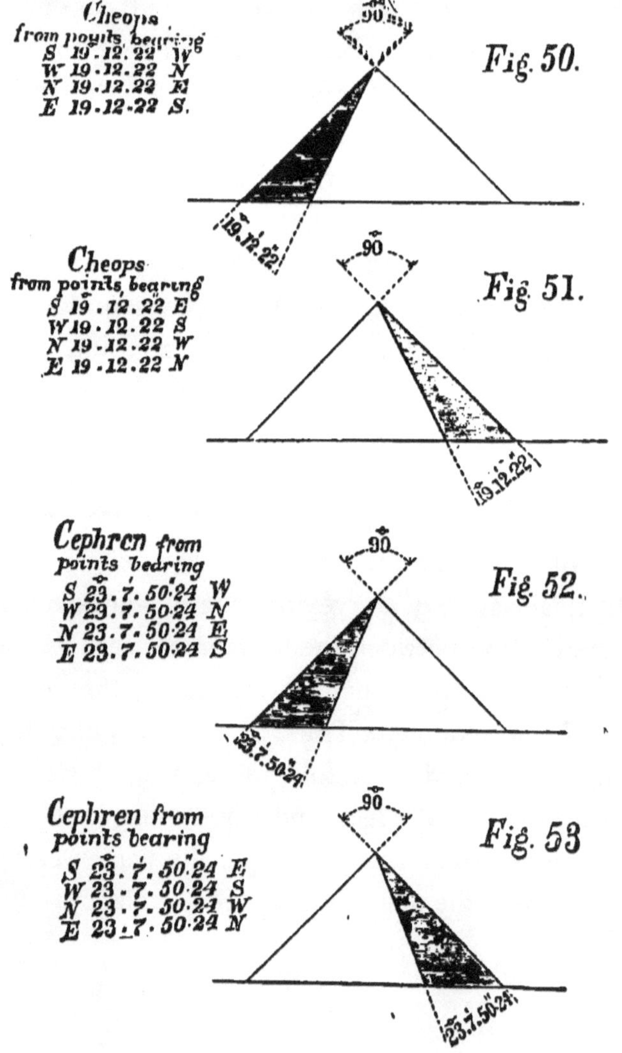

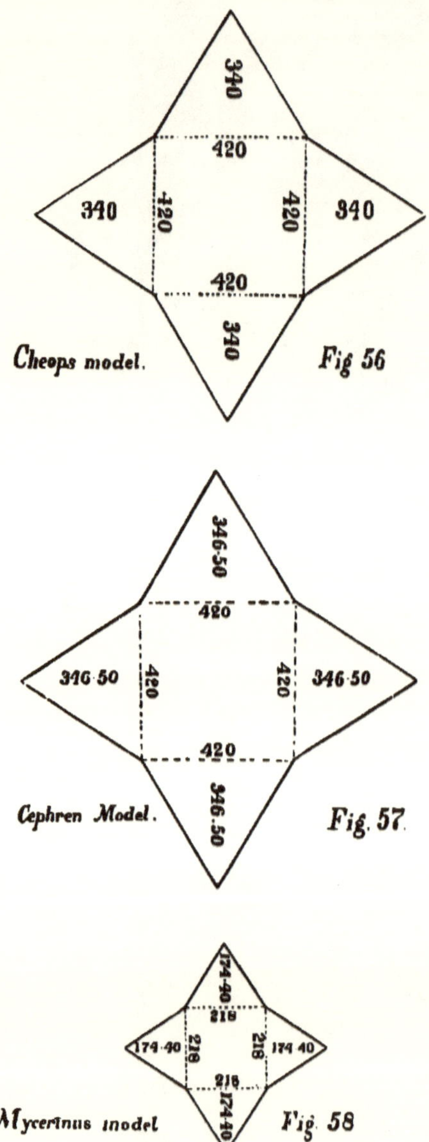

Cheops model. Fig 56

Cephren Model. Fig. 57

Mycerinus model Fig. 58

law, from which it will be seen that the Gïzeh surveyors

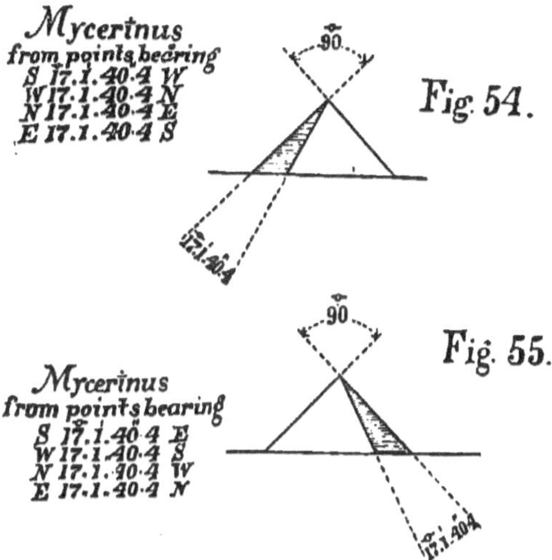

Fig. 54.

Fig. 55.

possessed, in this manner alone, eight distinctly defined bearings from each pyramid.

I recommend any one desirous to thoroughly comprehend these matters, to make a plan from my diagram, *Figure* 5, using R.B. cubits for measures, and to a suitable scale, on a piece of card-board. Then to cut out of the card-board the squares of the bases of the pyramids at the level of Cephren, viz., 420, 420 and 218 cubits respectively, for the three main pyramids. One hundred cubits to the inch is a convenient scale and within the limits of a sheet of Bath board.

By striking out the models on card-board in the manner shown by diagrams (*see Figures* 56, 57, and 58) they can be cut out with a penknife—cutting only *half through* where the lines are *dotted*—bent up together, and pasted along the edges with strips of writing paper about half an inch wide.

These models can be dropped into the squares cut out of the card-board plan, thus correcting the error caused by the thickness of the card-board base, and if placed in the sun, or at night by the light of *one* lamp or candle properly placed to represent the sun in the eastward or westward, the clear cut lines and clear contrasting shades will be manifest, and the lines illustrated by my figures can be identified.

When inspecting the model, it is well to bear in mind that the eye must be kept very nearly level with the table, or the pyramids will appear as if viewed from a balloon.

I believe that the stones were got up to the building by way of the north side of each pyramid. The casing on the south, east, and west, was probably built up as the work proceeded, and the whole of these three faces were probably thus finished and completed while there was not a single casing stone set on the north side. Then the work would be closed up until there remained nothing but a great gap or notch, wide at the bottom, and narrowing to the apex. The work on the north side would then be closed from the sides and top, and the bottom casing stone about the centre of the north side, would be the last stone set on the building.

These old builders were too expert not to have thus made use of all the shade which their own building would thus afford to a majority of the workmen.

Many of the obelisks were probably marks on pyramid lines of survey.

The pyramid indeed may have been a development of the obelisk for this purpose.

Their slanting sides might correspond with some of the nearly upright slant angles of the pyramids, in positions opposite certain lines. Reference to several of my figures will show how well this would come in.

Herodotus speaks of two obelisks at Heliopolis, and Bonwick tells us that Abd al Latif saw two there which he called Pharaoh's Needles. An Arab traveller, in 1190, saw a pyramid of copper on the summit of the one that remained, but it is now wanting. Pharaoh's Needles appear to have been situated about 20 miles NE. of the Gïzeh group, and their slope angles might have coincided with the apparent slope angles of Cephren or Cheops on the edge nearest the obelisk.

The ancient method of describing the meridian by means of the shadow of a ball placed on the summit of an obelisk points to a reasonable interpretation for the peculiar construction of the two pillars, Jachin and Boaz, which are said to have been situated in front of the Hebrew Temple at Jerusalem, and about which so much mysterious speculation has occurred.

They were no doubt used as sun-dials for the morning and afternoon sun by the shadow of the balls or "chapiters" thrown upon the pavement.

Without presuming to dispute the objects assigned by others for the galleries and passages which have been discovered in the pyramid Cheops, I venture to opine that they were employed to carry water to the builders. They are connected with a well, and the well with the Nile or canal. Whether the water was slided up the smooth galleries in boxes, or whether the cochlea, or water screw, was worked in them, their angles being suitable, it is impossible to conjecture; either plan would have been convenient and feasible.

These singular chambers and passages may indeed possibly have had to do with some hydraulic machinery of great power which modern science knows nothing about. The section of the pyramid, showing these galleries, in the pyramid books, has a most hydraulic appearance.

The tremendous strength and regularity of the cavities called the King's and Queen's chambers, the regularity and the *smallness* of most of the passages or massive stone connecting pipes, favor the idea that the chambers might have been reservoirs, their curious roofs, air chambers, and the galleries or passages, connecting pipes for working water under pressure. Water raised through the passages of this one pyramid nearest to the canal, might have been carried by troughs to the other pyramids, which were in all probability in course of construction at the same period of time. A profane friend of mine thinks that the sarcophagus or "sacred coffer" in the King's chamber may have been used by the chief architect and leading men of the works as a *bath*, and that the King's chamber was nothing more nor less than a delightful bath room.

The following quotation from the writing of an Arabian author (Ibn Abd Alkokm), is extracted from Bonwick's "Pyramid Facts and Fancies," page 72 :— "The Coptites mention in their books that upon them (the Pyramids) is an inscription engraven ; the exposition of it in Arabicke is this :—'I, Saurid the King built the Pyramids (in such and such a time), and finished them in six years ; he that comes after me, and says he is equal to me, let him destroy them in six hundred years ; and yet it is known that it is easier to pluck down than to build ; *and when I had finished them, I covered them with sattin, and let him cover them with slats.*'"

The italics are my own. The builder seems to have entertained the idea that his work would be partially destroyed, and afterwards temporarily repaired or rebuilt. The first part has unfortunately come true, and it is possible that the last part of the idea of King Saurid may be carried out, because it would not be so very expensive an undertaking for any civilized nation in the interest of science to re-case the pyramids of Gïzeh, so that they might be once more applied to land-surveying purposes in the ancient manner.

It would not be absolutely necessary to case the whole of the pyramid faces, so long as sufficient casing was put on to define the angles. The "*slats*" used might be a light wooden framework covered with thin metal. The metal should be painted white, except in the case of Mycerinus, which should be of a reddish color.

Main Triangular Dimensions of Plan are Represented by the Following Eight Right-angled Triangles.

TABLE TO EXPLAIN FIGURE 60.

AB	28		84		672	DG	3		72		576
BJ	45	× 3	135	× 8	1080	GE	4	× 24	96	× 8	768
JA	53		159		1272	ED	5		120		960
DC	3		135		1080	FW	48		48		384
CA	4	× 45	180	× 8	1440	WV	55	× 1	55	× 8	440
AD	5		225		1800	VF	73		73		584
EB	3		63		504	FB	20		80		640
BA	4	× 21	84	× 8	672	BA	21	× 4	84	× 8	672
AE	5		105		840	AF	29		116		928
FH	3		96		768						
HN	4	× 32	128	× 8	1024						
NF	5		160		1280						
AY	3		36		288						
YZ	4	× 12	48	× 8	384						
ZA	5		60		480						

NOTE.—In the above table the first column *is the Ratio*, the second *the connected Natural Numbers*, and the third column represents *the length of each line in R.B. cubits.*

§ 12. PRIMARY TRIANGLES AND THEIR SATELLITES; —OR THE ANCIENT SYSTEM OF RIGHT-ANGLED TRIGONOMETRY UNFOLDED BY A STUDY OF THE PLAN OF THE PYRAMIDS OF GIZEH.

Reference to *Fig.* 60 and the preceding table, will

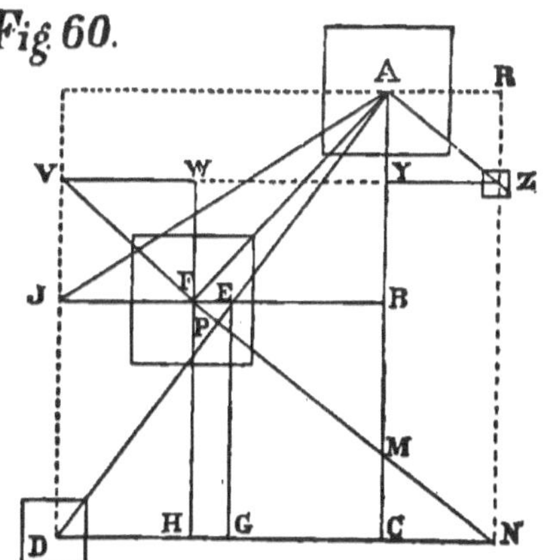

show that the main triangular dimensions of this plan (imperfect as it is from the lack of eleven pyramids) are represented by four main triangles, viz :—

	Ratio.
C A D C	3, 4, 5
F B A F	20, 21, 29
A B J A	28, 45, 53
F W V F	48, 55, 73

Figures 30 to 36 illustrate the two former, and *Figures* 61 and 62 illustrate the two latter. I will call triangles of this class "primary triangles," as the most suitable term, although it is applied to the main triangles of geodetic surveys.

We have only to select a number of such triangles and a system of trigonometry ensues, in which base, perpendicular, and hypotenuse of every triangle is a whole measure without fractions, and in which the nomenclature for every angle is clear and simple.

An angle of 43° 36′ 10·15″ will be called a 20, 21 angle, and an angle of 36° 52′ 11·65″ will be called a 3, 4 angle, and so on.

In the existing system whole angles, such as 40, 45, or 50 degrees, are surrounded by lines, most of which can only be described in numbers by interminable fractions.

In the ancient system, lines are only dealt with, and every angle in the table is surrounded by lines measuring whole units, and described by the use of a couple of simple numbers.

Connecting this with our present system of trigonometry would effect a saving in calculation, and general use of certain peculiar angles by means of which all the simplicity and beauty of the work of the ancients would be combined with the excellences of our modern instrumental appliances. Surveyors should appreciate the advantages to be derived from laying out traverses on the hypotenuses of "primary" triangles, by the saving of calculation and facility of plotting to be obtained from the practice.

The key to these old tables is the fact, that in "primary" triangles the right angled triangle formed by the sine and versed sine, also by the co-sine and co-versed-sine, is one in which base and perpendicular are measured by numbers without fractions. These I will call "satellite" triangles.

Thus, to the "primary" triangle 20, 21, 29, the ratios of the co-sinal and sinal satellites are respectively 7 to 3, and 2 to 5. (*See Figure* 35.) To the 48, 55, 73 triangle the satellites are 11, 5 and 8, 3 (*Fig.* 62); to the 3, 4, 5 triangle they are 2, 1 and 3, 1 (*Fig.* 30); and to the 28, 45, 53 triangle, they are 9, 5 and 7, 2 (*Fig.* 61). The

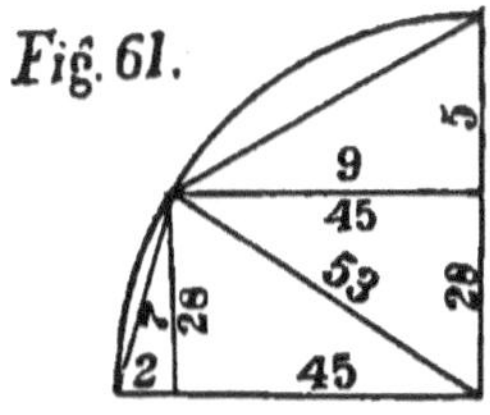

Fig. 61. The 28-45-53 *Triangle.*

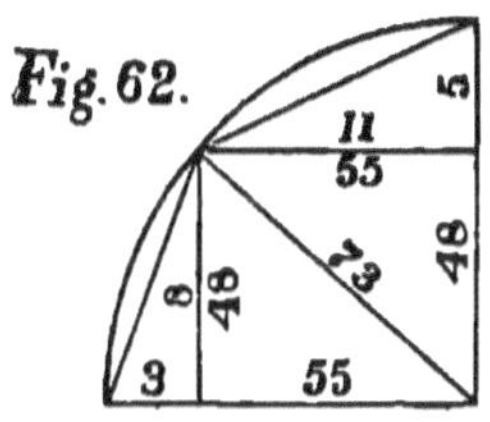

Fig. 62. The 48-55-73 *Triangle.*

primary triangle, 7, 24, 25, possesses as satellites the "primary" triangle, 3, 4, 5, and the ordinary triangle, 4, 1; and the primary triangle 41, 840, 841, is attended by the 20, 21, 29 triangle, as a satellite with the ordinary triangle 41, 1, and so on.

Since any ratio, however, whose terms, one or both, are represented by fractions, can be transformed into whole numbers, it evidently follows that every conceivable relative measure of two lines which we may decide to call co-sine and co-versed-sine, becomes a satellite to a corresponding "primary" triangle.

Now, since the angle of the satellite on the circumference must be *half* the angle of the adjacent primary triangle at the centre, it follows that in constructing a list of satellites and their angles, the angles of the corresponding primary triangles can be found. For instance—

Satellite 8, 3, contains 20° 33′ 21·76″
Satellite 2, 7, contains 15° 56′ 43·425″

Each of these angles doubled, gives the angle of a "primary" triangle as follows, viz. :-

The 48, 55, 73 triangle = 41° 6′ 43·52″
The 28, 45, 53 triangle = 31° 53′ 26·85″

The angles of the satellites together must always be 45°, because the angle at the circumference of a quadrant must always be 135°.

From the Gïzeh plan, as far as I have developed it, the following order of satellites begins to appear, which may be a guide to the complete Gïzeh plan ratio, and to those "primary" triangles in use by the pyramid surveyors in their ordinary work.

1, 2	2, 3	3, 4	4, 5	5, 6	6, 7	7, 8	8, 9
1, 3	2, 5	3, 5	4, 7	5, 7		7, 9	
1, 4	2, 7	3, 7	4, 9	5, 8			
1, 5	2, 9	3, 8		5, 9		7, 11	
1, 6				5, 11			
1, 7		3, 11		5, 13			
1, 8		3, 13					
1, 9							
1, 11							
1, 13							
1, 15							
1, 17							

Primary triangles may be found from the *angle of the satellite*, but it is an exceedingly round-about way. I will, however, give an example.

Let us construct a primary triangle from the satellite 4, 9.

$$\frac{\text{Rad.} \times 4}{9} = \cdot 4444444 = \text{Tangt.} \angle 23^\circ\ 57'\ 45\cdot 041''$$

$$\angle 23^\circ\ 57'\ 45\cdot 041'' \times 2 = 47^\circ\ 55'\ 30\cdot 083''.$$

therefore the angles of the "primary" are $47^\circ\ 55'\ 30\cdot 083''$.
and $42^\circ\ 4'\ 29\cdot 917''$.

The natural sine of $42^\circ\ 4'\ 29\cdot 917'' = \cdot 6701025$.

The natural co-sine $42^\circ\ 4'\ 29\cdot 917'' = \cdot 7422684$.

The greatest common measure of these numbers is about 102717, therefore—

Radius	10000000 ÷ 102717	= 97
Co-sine	7422684 ÷ 102717	= 72
Sine	6701025 ÷ 102717	= 65

and 65, 72, 97 is the primary triangle to which the satellites are 4, 9, and 5, 13. (*See Fig.* 63.) The figures

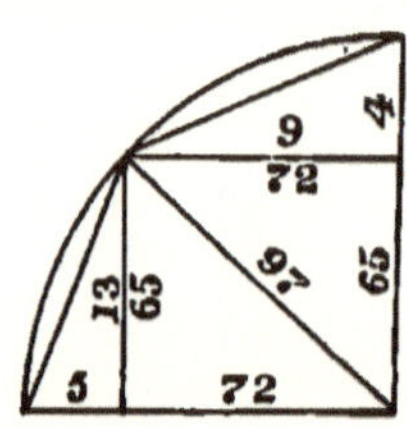

Fig. 63.

in the calculation do not balance exactly, in consequence of the insufficient delicacy of the tables or calculations.

The connection between primaries and satellites is shown by figure 64.

Fig. 64.

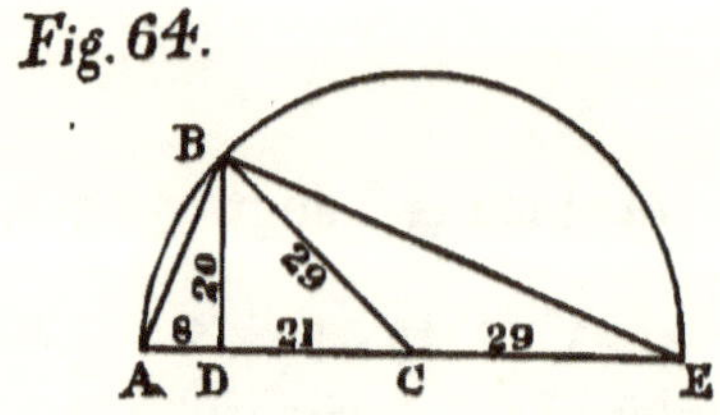

Let the triangle ADB be a satellite, 5, 2, which we will call BD 20, and AD 8. Let C be centre of semicircle ABE.

AD : DB :: DB : DE			= 50	(*Euc. VI.* 8)
AD + DE	= AE		= 58	= diameter
AE ÷ 2	= AC	= BC	= 29	= radius
AC − AD	= DC		= 21	= co-sine
	and DB		= 20	= sine

From the preceding it is manifest that—

$$\frac{\text{sine}^2}{\text{ver-s}} + \text{ver-s} = \text{dia.}$$

The formula to find the "primary triangle" to any satellite is as follows :—

Let the long ratio line of the satellite or sine be called *a*, and the short ratio line or versed-sine be called *b*. Then—

$$(1)\quad a = \text{sine,}$$

$$(2)\quad \frac{a^2 + b^2}{2b} = \text{radius.}$$

$$(3)\quad \frac{a^2 - b^2}{2b} = \text{co-sine.}$$

Therefore various primary triangles can be constructed on a side DB (*Fig.* 64) as sine, by taking different measures for AD as versed-sine.

For example—

From Satellite 5, 1.

$$5 = \text{sine} = 5$$

$$\frac{5^2 + 1^2}{2 \times 1} = \text{radius} = 13$$

$$\frac{5^2 - 1^2}{2 \times 1} = \text{co-s.} = 12$$

From Satellite 5, 2.	5	= sine = 5	× 4	20
	$\frac{5^2 + 2^2}{2 \times 2}$	= radius = $7\frac{1}{4}$		29
	$\frac{5^2 - 2^2}{2 \times 2}$	= co-s. = $5\frac{1}{4}$		21

Finally arises the following simple rule for the construction of "primaries" to contain any angle—*Decide upon a satellite which shall contain half the angle*—say, 5, 1. Call the first figure *a*, the second *b*, then—

$$a^2 + b^2 = \text{hypotenuse.}$$
$$a^2 - b^2 = \text{perpendicular.}$$
$$a \times 2b = \text{base.}$$

			"PRIMARY"	LOWEST RATIO.
Thus— Satellite 5, 1	$5^2 + 1^2$	=	26	= 13
	$5^2 - 1^2$	=	24	= 12
	$5 \times 2 \times 1$	=	10	= 5
and— Satellite 5, 2	$5^2 + 2^2$	=	29	= 29
	$5^2 - 2^2$	=	21	= 21
	$5 \times 2 \times 2$	=	20	= 20

Having found the lowest ratio of the three sides of a "primary" triangle, the lowest whole numbers for tangent, secant, co-secant, and co-tangent, if required, are obtained in the following manner.

Take for example the 20, 21, 29 triangle, now $20 \times 21 = 420$, and $29 \times 420 = 12180$, a new radius instead of 29 from which with the sine 20, and co-sine 21, increased in the same ratio, the whole canon of the 20, 21, 29 triangle will come out in whole numbers.

Similarly in the triangle 48, 55, 73, radius 73 × 13200 (the product of 48 × 55) makes radius in whole numbers 963600, for an even canon without fractions. This is because sine and co-sine are the two denominators in the fractional parts of the other lines when worked out at the lowest ratio of sine, co-sine, and radius.

After I found that the plan of the Gïzeh group was a system of "primary" triangles, I had to work out the rule for constructing them, for I had never met with it in any book, but I came across it afterwards in the "Penny Encyclopedia," and in Rankine's "Civil Engineering."

The practical utility of these triangles, however, does not appear to have received sufficient consideration. I certainly never met with any except the 3, 4, 5, in the practice of any surveyor of my acquaintance.

(For squaring off a line nothing could be more convenient than the 20, 21, 29 triangle; for instance, taking a base of 40 links, then using the whole chain for the two remaining sides of 42 and 58 links.)

Table of Some Primary Triangles and their Satellites.

ANGLE OF PRIMARY			PRIMARY			SATELLITE.		ANGLE OF SATELLITE		
DEG.	MIN.	SEC.	RAD.	CO.-S.	SINE.			DEG.	MIN.	SEC.
2	47	39·70	841	840	41	41	1	1	23	49·85
6	43	58·62	145	144	17	17	1	3	21	59·31
8	47	50·69	85	84	13	13	1	4	23	55·34
10	23	19·89	61	60	11	11	1	5	11	39·94
12	40	49·37	41	40	9	9	1	6	20	24·68
14	14	59·10	65	63	16	8	1	7	7	29·55
16	15	36·73	25	24	7	7	1	8	7	48·36
18	55	28·71	37	35	12	6	1	9	27	44·35
22	37	11·51	13	12	5	5	1	11	18	35·75
25	3	27·27	85	77	36	9	2	12	31	43·63
25	59	21·22	89	80	39	13	3	12	59	40·61
28	4	20·94	17	15	8	4	1	14	2	10·47
30	30	36·49	65	56	33	11	3	15	15	18·24
31	53	26·85	53	45	28	7	2	15	56	43·42
36	52	11·65	5	4	3	3	1	18	26	5·82
41	6	43·52	73	55	48	8	3	20	33	21·76
42	4	30·08	97	72	65	13	5	21	2	15·04
43	36	10·15	29	21	20	5	2	21	48	5·07

Table of some Primary Triangles and their Satellites.

(Continued.)

ANGLE OF PRIMARY			PRIMARY			SATELLITE.		ANGLE OF SATELLITE		
DEG.	MIN.	SEC.	RAD.	CO.-S.	SINE.			DEG.	MIN.	SEC.
46	23	49·85	29	20	21	7	3	23	11	54·92
47	55	29·92	97	65	72	9	4	23	57	44·96
48	53	16·48	73	48	55	11	5	24	26	38·24
53	7	48·35	5	3	4	2	1	26	33	54·17
58	6	33·15	53	28	45	9	5	29	3	16·57
59	29	23·51	65	33	56	7	4	29	44	41·75
61	55	39·06	17	8	15	5	3	30	57	49·53
64	0	38·78	89	39	80	8	5	32	0	19·39
64	56	32·73	85	36	77	11	7	32	28	16·36
67	22	48·49	13	5	12	3	2	33	41	24.24
71	4	31·29	37	12	35	7	5	35	32	15·64
73	44	23·27	25	7	24	4	3	36	52	11·63
75	45	0·90	65	16	63	9	7	37	52	30·45
77	19	10·63	41	9	40	5	4	38	39	35·31
79	36	40·11	61	11	60	6	5	39	48	20·05
81	12	9·31	85	13	84	7	6	40	36	4·65
83	16	1·38	145	17	144	9	8	41	38	0·69
87	12	20·30	841	41	840	21	20	43	36	10·15

Reference to the plan ratio table at the commencement, and to the tables here introduced, will shew that most of the primary triangles mentioned are indicated on the plan ratio table principally by the lines corresponding to the ratios of the satellites. Thus—

PRIMARY TRIANGLE	INDICATED BY
17, 144, 145.	Triangle FP, PA, AF on plan.
13, 84, 85.	Plan ratio of SJ to SU, 7 to 6.
11, 60, 61.	Plan ratio BC to FB, 6 to 5, and DN to NR, 61 to 60.
12, 35, 37.	Plan ratio EO to AY, 37 to 12, and EA to AY, 35 to 12.
5, 12, 13.	Plan ratio CY to BC, 3 to 2; JE to EX, 3 to 2; CA to YA, 5 to 1; and NZ to ZA, 12 to 5.
8, 15, 17.	Plan ratio FB to BY, 5 to 3, and AC to BC, 15 to 8.
33, 56, 55.	Plan ratio YX to AY, 7 to 4; AB to BO, 7 to 4; and EA to AZ, 7 to 4.
28, 45, 53.	Exists on plan, AB, BJ, JA.
3, 4, 5.	Pervades the plan, and is also indicated by plan ratio GX to DG, 2 to 1; SU to SV, 2 to 1; and CY to YZ, 3 to 1.
48, 55, 73.	Exists on plan, FW, WV, VF—and is also indicated by plan ratio FO to OZ, 8 to 3.
65, 72, 97.	Plan ratio AC to CH, 9 to 4; MY to YZ, 9 to 4.
20, 21, 29.	Exists on plan FB, BA, AF; and plan ratio, GU to DG, 5 to 2.

It seems probable that could I add to my pyramid plan the lines and triangles that the missing eleven pyramids would supply, it would comprise a complete table on which would appear indications of all the ratios and triangles made use of in right-angled trigonometry, a "*ratiometer*," in fact.

I firmly believe that so far as I have gone it is correct—and it is possible, therefore, with the start that I have made, for others to continue the work, and add the eleven pyramids to the plan in their correct geometrical position. By continuing the system of evolution by which I defined the position of Cephren, and the little pyramid to the south-east of Cheops, after I had obtained Cheops and Mycerinus, may be rebuilt, at one and the same time, a skeleton of the trigonometrical tables of a forgotten civilization, and the plan of those pyramids which are its only link with the present age.

§ 13. THE SIZE AND SHAPE OF THE PYRAMIDS INDICATED BY THE PLAN.

I pursued my investigations into the slopes and altitudes of the pyramids without reference to the plan, after once deciding their exact bases.

Now it will be interesting to note some of the ways in which the plan hints at the shape and size of these pyramids, and corroborates my work.

The dimensions of *Cheops* are indicated on the plan by the lines EA to YA, measuring 840 and 288 R.B. cubits respectively, being the half periphery of its horizontal section at the level of Cephren's base, and its own altitude from its own base. (*See Fig.* 5.)

The line EA, in fact, represents in R.B. cubits the half periphery of the bases of either Cheops or Cephren measured at the level which I have set forth as the *plan level,* viz., base of Cephren.

The ratio of Cephren's base to Cephren's altitude is indicated on the plan by the ratios of the lines BC to EB, or FO to OR, viz., 32 to 21. (*See Fig.* 4.)

The altitude of Mycerinus above Cephren's base appears on plan in the line EF, measuring 136 R.B. cubits.

The line EO on plan measures 888 cubits, which would be the length of a line stretched from the apex of Cheops to the point E, at the level of Cheops' base.

This merits consideration:—the lines EA and AY are connected on plan at the centre of Cheops, and the lines EO and EA are connected on plan at the point E.

Now the lines EO, EA and AY are sides of a "primary triangle," whose ratio is 37, 35, 12, and whose measure in cubits is 888, 840, and 288; and if we suppose the line EA to be stretched horizontally beneath the pyramids at the level of the base of Cheops from E to A on plan, and the line AY to be a plumb line hanging from the apex of Cheops to the level of his base, then will the line EO just stretch from the point E to the apex of Cheops, and the three lines will connect the two main pyramids by a vertical triangle of which EA, AY and EO form the base, perpendicular, and hypotenuse. Or, to explain it in another manner: let the line EA be a *cord* stretching horizontally from A at the centre of the base of Cheops to the point E, both ends being at the same level; let the line AY be a *rod*, lift it on the end A till it stands erect, then is the end Y the apex of Cheops, Now, the line EO would just stretch from the top of the rod AY to the point E first described.

It is a singular coincidence, and one that may be interesting to students of the *interior* of the Pyramids, that the side EP, of the small 3, 4, 5 triangle, EP, PF, FE, in the centre of the plan, measures 81·60 R.B. cubits, which is very nearly eight times the "*true breadth*" of the King's chamber in Cheops, according to Piazzi Smyth; for $\frac{81 \cdot 60}{8} = 10 \cdot 20$ R.B. cubits, or 206·046 pyramid inches (one R.B. cubit being 20·2006 pyramid inches). The sides of this little triangle measure 81·60, 108·80, and 136, R.B. cubits respectively, as can be easily proved from the plan ratio table.

§ 14. A SIMPLE INSTRUMENT FOR LAYING OFF "PRIMARY TRIANGLES."

A simple instrument for laying off "primary triangles" upon the ground, might have been made with three rods divided into a number of small equal divisions, with holes through each division, which rods could be pinned together triangularly, the rods working as arms on a flat table, and the pins acting as pointers or sights.

One of the pins would be permanently fixed in the table through the first hole of two of the rods or arms, and the two other pins would be movable so as to fix the arms into the shape of the various "primary triangles."

Thus with the two main arms pinned to the cross arm in the 21st and 29th hole from the permanently pinned end, with the cross arm stretched to twenty divisions, a 20, 21, 29 triangle would be the result, and so on.

§14*a*. GENERAL OBSERVATIONS.

I must be excused by geometricians for going so much in detail into the simple truths connected with right-angled trigonometry. My object has been to make it very clear to that portion of the public not versed in geometry, that the Pyramids of Egypt must have been used for land surveying by right-angled triangles with sides having whole numbers.

A re-examination of these pyramids on the ground with the ideas suggested by the preceding pages in view, may lead to interesting discoveries.

For instance, it is just possible that the very accurately and beautifully worked stones in the walls of the King's chamber of Cheops, may be found to indicate the ratios of the rectangles formed by the bases and perpendiculars of the triangulations used by the old surveyors—that on these walls may be found, in fact, corroboration of the theory that I have set forth. I am led to believe also from the fact that Gïzeh was a central and commanding locality, and that it was the custom of those who preceded those Egyptians that history tells of, to excavate mighty caverns in the earth—that, therefore, in the limestone upon which the pyramids are built, and underneath the pyramids, may be found vast excavations, chambers and galleries, that had entrance on the face of the ridge at the level of High Nile. From this subterraneous city, occupied by the priests and the surveyors of Memphis, access may be found to every pyramid; and while to the outside world the pyramids might have appeared sealed up as mausoleums to the Kings that it may have seen publicly interred therein, this very sealing and closing of the outer galleries may have only rendered their mysterious recesses more private to the priests who entered from below, and who were, perhaps, enabled to ascend by private passages to their very summits. The recent discovery of a number of regal mummies stowed away in an out of the way cave on the banks of the Nile, points to the unceremonious manner in which the real rulers of Kings and people may have dealt with their sovereigns, the pomp and circumstance of a public burial once over. It is just possible that the chambers in the pyramids may have been used in connection with their mysteries: and the small passages called by some "ventilators" or "air passages," sealed as they were from the chamber by a thin stone (and therefore no ventilators) may have been *auditory passages* along which sound might have been projected from other chambers not yet opened by the moderns; 'sounds which were perhaps a part of the "hanky panky" of the ancient ceremonial connected with the "mysteries" or the "religion" of that period.

Down that "well" which exists in the interior of Cheops, and in the limestone foundations of the pyramid, should I be disposed to look for openings into the vast subterraneous chambers which I am convinced *do* exist below the Pyramids of Gïzeh.

The priests of the Pyramids of Lake Mœris had their vast subterranean residences. It appears to me more than probable that those of Gïzeh were similarly provided. And I go further:—Out of these very caverns may have been excavated the limestone of which the pyramids were built, thus killing two birds with one stone—building the instruments and finding cool quarters below for those who were to make use of them. In the bowels of that limestone ridge on which the pyramids are built will yet be found, I feel convinced, ample information as to their uses. A good diamond drill with two or three hundred feet of rods is what is what is wanted to test this, and the solidity of the pyramids at the same time.

§ 15. PRIMARY TRIANGULATION.

Primary triangulation would be useful to men of almost every trade and profession in which tools or instruments are used. Any one might in a short time construct a table for himself answering to every degree or so in the circumference of a circle for which only forty or fifty triangles are required.

It would be worth while for some one to print and publish a correct set of these tables embracing a close division of the circle, in which set there should be a column showing the angle in degrees, minutes, seconds and decimals, and also a column for the satellite, thus—

SATELLITE.		PRIMARY.			ANGLE.
5	2	20	21	29	43° 36′ 10·15″
7	3	21	20	29	46° 23′ 49·85″

and so on. Such a set of tables would be a boon to sailors, architects, surveyors, engineers, and all handicraftsmen: and I make bold to say, would assist in the intricate investigations of the astronomer:—and the rule for building the tables is so simple, that they could easily be achieved. The architect from these tables might arrange the shape of his chambers, passages or galleries, so that all measures, not only at right angles on the walls, but from any corner of floor to ceiling should be even feet. The pitch of his roofs might be more varied, and the monotony of the buildings relieved, with rafters and tie-beams always in even measures. The one solitary 3, 4, 5 of Vitruvius would cease to be his standard for a staircase; and even in doors and sashes, and panels of glass, would he be alive to the perfection of rectitude gained by evenly-measured diagonals. By a slight modification of the compass card, the navigator of blue water might steer his courses on the hypotenuses of great primary triangles—such tables would be useful to all sailors and surveyors who have to deal with latitude and departure. For instance, familiarity with such tables would make ever present in the mind of the surveyor or sailor his proportionate northing and easting, no matter what course he was steering between north and east, "the *primary*" embraces *the three ideas in one view.*

In designing trussed roofs or bridges, the "primaries" would be invaluable to the engineer, strain-calculations on diagonal and upright members would be simplified, and the builder would find the benefit of a measure in even feet or inches from centre of one pin or connection to another.

For earthwork slopes 3, 4, 5; 20, 21, 29; 21, 20, 29; and 4, 3, 5 would be found more convenient ratios than 1 *to* 1, and 1½ *to* 1, etc. Templates and battering rules would be more perfect and correct, and the engineer could prove his slopes and measure his work at one and the same time without the aid of a staff or level; the slope measures would reveal the depth, and the slope measures and bottom width would be all the measures required, while the top width would prove the correctness of the slopes and the measurements.

To the land surveyor, however, the primary triangle would be the most useful, and more especially to those laying out new holdings, whether small or large, in new countries.

Whether it be for a "squatter's run," or for a town allotment, the advantages of a diagonal measure to every parallelogram in even *miles*, *chains*, or *feet*, should be keenly felt and appreciated.

This was, I believe, *one* of the secrets of the speedy and correct replacement of boundary marks by the Egyptian land surveyors.

I have heard of a review in the "Contemporary," September, 1881, referring to the translation of a papyrus in the British Museum, by Dr. Eisenlohr—"*A handbook of practical arithmetic and geometry,*" *etc.*, "*such as we might suppose would be used by a scribe acting as clerk of the works, or by an architect to shew the working out of the problems he had to solve in his operations.*" I should like to see a translation of the book, from which it appears that "*the clumsiness of the Egyptian method is very remarkable.*" Perhaps this Egyptian "*Handbook,*" may yet shew that their operations were not so "*clumsy,*" as they appear at first sight to those accustomed to the practice of modern trigonometry. I may not have got the exact "hang" of the Egyptian method of land surveying—for I do not suppose that even their "clumsy" method is to be got at intuitively; but I claim that I have shewn how the Pyramids could be used for that purpose, and that the subsidiary instrument described by me was practicable.

I claim, therefore, that the theory I have set up, that the pyramids were the theodolites of the Egyptians, is sound. That the ground plan of these pyramids discloses a beautiful system of primary triangles and satellites I think I have shown beyond the shadow of a doubt; and that this system of geometric triangulation or right-angled trigonometry was the method practised, seems in the preceding pages to be fairly established. I claim, therefore, that I have discovered and described the main secret of the pyramids, that I have found for them at last a practical use, and that it is no longer "*a marvel how after the annual inundation, each property could have been accurately described by the aid of geometry.*" I have advanced nothing in the shape of a theory that will not stand a practical test; but to do it, the pyramids should be *re-cased.* Iron sheeting, on iron or wooden framework, would answer. I may be wrong in some of my conclusions, but in the main I am satisfied that I am right. It must be admitted that I have worked under difficulties; a glimpse at the pyramids three and twenty years ago, and the meagre library of a nomad in the Australian wilderness having been all my advantages, and time at my disposal only that snatched from the rare intervals of leisure afforded by an arduous professional life.

After fruitless waiting for a chance of visiting Egypt and Europe, to sift the matter to the bottom, I have at last resolved to give my ideas to the world as they stand; crude necessarily, so I must be excused if in some details I may be found erroneous; there is truth I know in the general conclusions. I am presumptuous enough to believe that the R.B. cubit of 1·685 British feet was the measure of the pyramids of Gïzeh, although there may have been an astronomical 25 inch cubit also. It appears to me that no cubit measure to be depended on is either to be got from a stray measuring stick found in the joints of a ruined building, or from any line or dimensions of one of the pyramids. I submit that a most reasonable way to get a cubit measure out of the Pyramids of Gïzeh, was to do as I did :—take them as a whole, comprehend and establish the general ground plan, find it geometric and harmonic, obtain the ratios of all the lines, establish a complete set of natural and even numbers to represent the measures of the lines, and finally bring these numbers to cubits by a common multiplier (which in this case was the number eight). After the whole proportions had been thus expressed in a cubit évolved *from* the whole proportions, I established its length in British feet by dividing the base of Cephren, as known, by the number of my cubits representing its base. It is pretty sound evidence of the theory being correct that this test, with 420 cubits neat for Cephren, gave me also a neat measure for Cheops, from Piazzi Smyth's base, of 452 cubits, and that at the same level, these two pyramids become equal based.

I have paid little attention to the inside measurements. I take it we should first obtain our exoteric knowledge before venturing on esotoric research. Thus the intricate internal measurements of Cheops, made by various enquirers have been little service to me, while the accurate measures of the base of Cheops by Piazzi Smyth, and John James Wild's letter to Lord Brougham, helped me amazingly, as from the two I established the plan level and even bases of Cheops and Cephren at plan level—as I have shown in the preceding pages. My theory demanded that both for the building of the pyramids and for the construction of the models or subsidiary instruments of the surveyors, simple slope ratios should govern each building; before I conclude, I shall show how I got at my slope ratios, by evolving them from the general ground plan.

I am firmly convinced that a careful investigation into the ground plans of the various other groups of pyramids will amply confirm my survey theory—the relative positions of the groups should also be established—much additional light will be then thrown on the subject.

Let me conjure the investigator to view these piles *from a distance* with his mind's eye, as the old surveyors viewed them with their bodily eye. Approach them too nearly, and, like Henry Kinglake, you will be lost in the "*one idea of solid immensity.*" Common sense tells us they were built to be viewed from a distance.

Modern surveyors stand *near* their instruments, and send their flagmen to a distance; the Egyptian surveyor was *one of his own flagmen*, and his instruments were towering to the skies on the distant horizon. These mighty tools will last out many a generation of surveyors.

The modern astronomer from the top of an observatory points his instruments direct at the stars; the Egyptian astronomer from the summit of his particular pyramid directed his observations to the rising and setting of the stars, or the positions of the heavenly bodies in respect to the far away groups of pyramids scattered around him in the distance; and by comparing notes, and with the knowledge of the relative position of the groups, did these observers map out the sky. Solar and lunar shadows of their own pyramids on the flat trenches prepared for the purpose, enabled the astronomer at each observatory to record the annual and monthly flight of time, while its hours were marked by the shadows of their obelisks, capped by copper pyramids or balls, on the more delicate pavements of the court-yards of their public buildings.

We must grasp that their celestial and terrestrial surveys were almost a reverse process to our own, before we can venture to enquire into its details. It then becomes a much easier tangle to unravel. That a particular pyramid among so many, should have been chosen as a favoured interpreter of Divine truths, seems an unfair conclusion to the other pyramids;—that the other pyramids were rough and imperfect imitations, appears to my poor capacity "a base and impotent conclusion;"—(as far as I can learn, *Mycerinus*, in its perfection, was a marvel of the mason's art;) but that one particular pyramid should have anything to do with the past or the future of the lost ten tribes of Israel (whoever that fraction of our present earthly community may be), seems to me the wildest conclusion of all, except perhaps the theory that this one pyramid points to the future of the British race. Yet in one way do I admit that the pyramids point to our future.

Thirty-six centuries ago, they, already venerable with antiquity, looked proudly down on living labouring Israel, in helpless slavery, in the midst of an advanced civilization, of which the history, language, and religion are now forgotten, or only at best, slightly understood.

Thirty-six centuries hence, they may look down on a civilization equally strange, in which our history, language, and religion, Hebrew race, and British race, may have no place, no part.

If the thoughts of noble poets live, as they seem to do, old Cheops, that mountain of massive masonry, may (like the brook of our Laureate), in that dim future, still be singing, as he seems to sing now, this idea, though not perhaps these words:

> "For men may come, and men may go,
> But I go on for ever."

"Ars longa, vita brevis." Man's work remains, when the workman is forgotten; fair work and square, can never perish entirely from men's minds, so long as the world stands. These pyramids were grand and noble works, and they will not perish till their reputation has been re-established in the world, when they will live in men's memories to all generations as symbols of the mighty past. To the minds of many now, as to Josephus in his day, they are "*vast and vain monuments,*" records of folly. To me they are as monuments of peace, civilization and order—relics of a people living under wise and beneficent rulers—evidences of cultivation, science, and art.

§ 16. THE PENTANGLE OR FIVE POINTED STAR THE GEOMETRIC SYMBOL OF THE GREAT PYRAMID.

From time immemorial this symbol has been a blazing pointer to grand and noble truths, and a solemn emblem of important duties.

Its geometric significance, however, has long been lost sight of.

It is said to have constituted the seal or signet of King Solomon (1000 B.C.), and in early times it was in use among the Jews, as a symbol of safety.

It was the Pentalpha of Pythagoras, and the Pythagorean emblem of health (530 B.C.).

It was carried as the banner of Antiochus, King of Syria (surnamed Soter, or the Preserver), in his wars against the Gauls (260 B.C.). Among the Cabalists, the star with the sacred name written on each of its points, and in the centre, was considered talismanic; and in ancient times it was employed all over Asia as a charm against witchcraft. Even now, European troops at war with Arab tribes, sometimes find, under the clothing, on the breasts of their slain enemies, this ancient emblem, in the form of a metal talisman, or charm.

The European Göethe puts these words into the mouth of Mephistopheles:

> "I am hindered egress by a quaint device upon the threshold, —that five-toed damned spell."

I shall set forth the geometric significance of this star, as far as my general subject warrants me, and show that it is the *geometric emblem of extreme and mean ratio*, and the *symbol of the Egyptian Pyramid Cheops.*

A plane geometric star, or a solid geometric pyramid, may be likened to the corolla of a flower, each separate side representing a petal. With its petals opened and exposed to view, the flower appears in all its glorious beauty; but when closed, many of its beauties are hidden. The botanist seeks to view it flat or open in its geometric symmetry, and also closed, as a bud, or in repose :—yet judges and appreciates the one state from the other. In the same manner must we deal with the five pointed star, and also with the Pyramid Cheops.

In dealing with so quaint a subject, I may be excused, in passing, for the quaint conceit of likening the interior galleries and chambers of this pyramid to the interior whorl of a flower, stamens and pistil, mysterious and incomprehensible.

Figure 67 (page 101), is the five pointed star, formed by the unlapping of the five slant sides of a pyramid with a pentagonal base.

Figure 70 (page 106), is a star formed by the unlapping of the four slant sides of the pyramid Cheops.

The pentagon GFRHQ, (*Fig.* 67) is the base of the pyramid "*Pentalpha*," and the triangles EGF, BFR, ROH, HNQ and QAG, represent the five sides, so that supposing the lines GF, FR, RH, HQ and QG, to be hinges connecting these sides with the base, then by lifting the sides, and closing them in, the points A, E, B, O, and N, would meet over the centre C.

Thus do we close the geometric flower Pentalpha, and convert it into a pyramid.

In the same manner must we lift the four slant sides of the pyramid Cheops from its star development, (*Fig*. 70) and close them in, the four points meeting over the centre of the base, forming the solid pyramid. Such transitions point to the indissoluble connection between plane and solid geometry.

As the *geometric emblem of extreme and mean ratio*, the pentangle appears as an assemblage of lines divided the one by the others *in extreme and mean ratio.*

To explain to readers not versed in geometry, what extreme and mean ratio signifies, I refer to Figure 65 :—

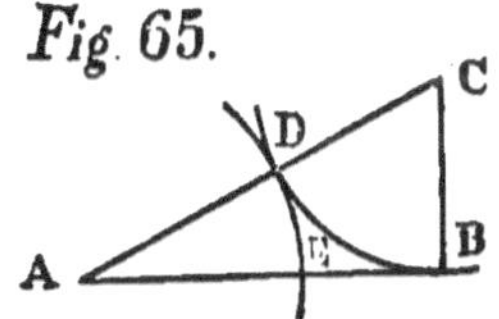

Fig. 65.

Let AB be the given line to be divided in extreme and mean ratio, *i.e.*, so that the whole line may be to the greater part, as the greater is to the less part.

Draw BC perpendicular to AB, and equal to half AB. Join AC; and with BC as a radius from C as a centre, describe the arc DB; then with centre A, and radius

AD, describe the arc DE; so shall AB be divided in E, in extreme and mean ratio, or so that AB : AE : : AE : EB. (Note that AE is equal to the side of a decagon inscribed in a circle with radius AB.)

Let it be noted that since the division of a line in mean and extreme ratio is effected by means of the 2, 1 triangle, ABC, therefore, as the exponent of this ratio, another reason presents itself why it should be so important a feature in the Gïzeh pyramids in addition to its connection with the primary triangle 3, 4, 5.

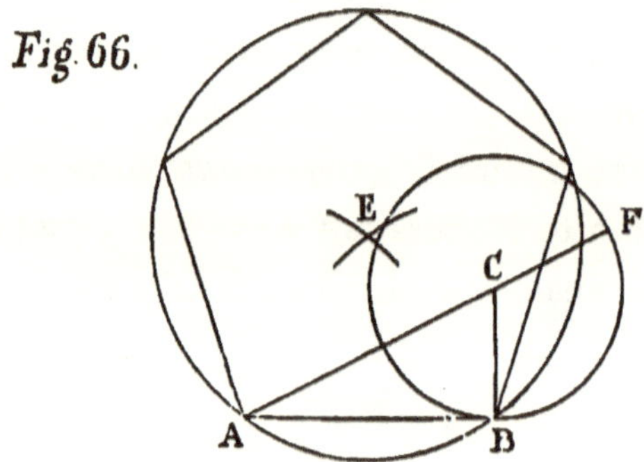

Fig. 66.

To complete the explanation offered with figure 65, I must refer to Fig. 66, where in constructing a pentagon, the 2, 1 triangle ABC, is again made use of.

The line AB is a side of the pentagon. The line BC is a perpendicular to it, and half its length. The line AC is produced to F, CF being made equal to CB; then with B as a centre, and radius BF, the arc at E is described; and with A as a centre, and the same radius, the arc at E is intersected, their intersection being the centre of the circle circumscribing the pentagon, and upon which the remaining sides are laid off.

We will now refer to figure 67, in which the pentangle appears as the symbolic exponent of the division of lines in extreme and mean ratio.

Thus: MC : MH : : MH : HC
AF : AG : : AG : GF
AB : AF : : AF : FB

while MN, MH or XC : CD : : 2 : 1—being the geometric template of the work.

Thus every line in this beautiful symbol by its intersections with the other lines, manifests the problem. Note also that

GH = GA
AE = AF
DH = DE

I append a table showing the comparative measures of the lines in Fig. 67, taking radius of the circle as a million units.

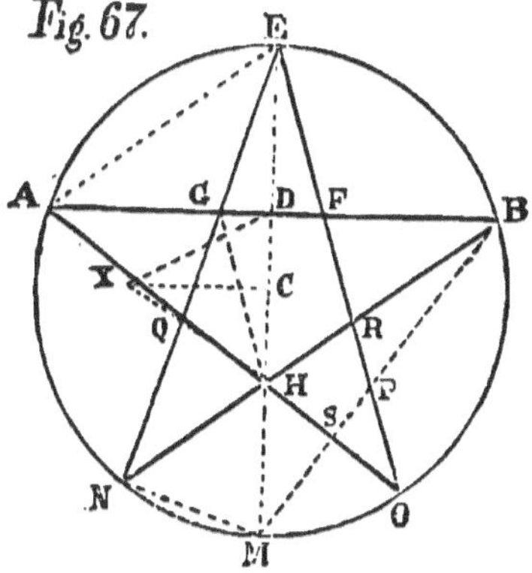

Fig. 67.

Table Showing the Comparative Measures of Lines.

(*Fig*. 67.)

ME = 2000000 = diameter.
AB = 1902113 = AD + DB
MB = 1618034 = MC + MH = MP + PB
AS = 1538841·5
EP = 1453086 = AG + FB
AF = 1175570 = AE = GB
MC = 1000000 = radius = CD + DX = CH + CX
AD = 951056·5 = DB = DS
PB = 854102
QS = 812298·5
MP = 763932 = CH × 2 = base of Cheops.
AG = 726543 = GH = XH = HN = PF = FB = Slant edge of Cheops. = slant edge of Pent. Pyr.
DE = 690983 = DH = XD = apothem of Pentagonal Pyramid.
MH = 618034 = MN = XC = { apothem of Cheops. altitude of Pentagonal Pyramid. side of decagon inscr'd in circle.
MS = 500000
485868 = { mean proportional between MH and HC altitude of Cheops.
OP = 449027 = GF = GD + DF
HC = 381966 = half base of Cheops.
SO = 363271·5 = HS
CD = 309017 = half M H
PR = 277516
GD = 224513·5
SP = 263932

The triangle DXH represents a vertical section of the pentagonal pyramid; the edge HX is equal to HN, and the apothem DX is equal to DE. Let DH be a hinge attaching the plane DXH to the base, now lift the plane DXH until the point X is vertical above the centre C. Then the points A, E, B, O, N of the five slant slides, when closed up, will all meet at the point X over the centre C.

We have now built a pyramid out of the pentangle, whose slope is 2 to 1, altitude CX being to CD as 2 to 1.

Apothem DX = DE
Altitude CX = HM or MN
Altitude CX + CH = CM radius.
Apothem DX + CD = CM radius.
Edge HX = HN or PF

Note also that

$$\frac{MP}{2} = CH$$

$$OP = HR$$

Let us now consider *the Pentangle as the symbol of the Great Pyramid Cheops.*

The line MP = the base of Cheops.
The line CH = half base of Cheops.
The line HM = apothem of Cheops.
The line HN = slant edge of Cheops.

Thus: Apothem of Cheops = side of decagon.
Apothem of Cheops = altitude of pentagonal pyramid.

Slant edge of Cheops = slant edge of pentagonal pyramid.

Now since apothem of Cheops = MH

and half base of Cheops = HC

then do apothem and half base represent, when taken together, extreme and mean ratio, and altitude is a mean proportional between them: it having already been stated, which also is proved by the figures in the table, that MC : MH : : MH : HC and apoth : alt : : alt : half base.

Thus is the four pointed star *Cheops* evolved from the five pointed star *Pentalpha*. This is shown clearly by Fig. 68, thus:—

Fig. 68.

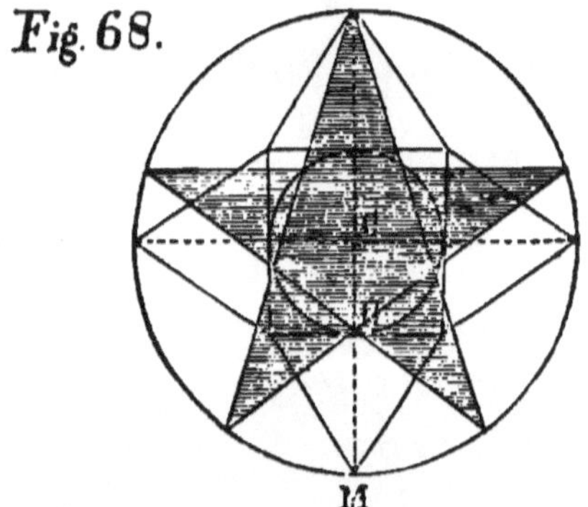

Within a circle describe a pentangle, around the interior pentagon of the star describe a circle, around the circle describe a square; then will the square represent the base of Cheops.

Draw two diameters of the outer circle passing through the centre square at right angles to each other, and each diameter parallel to sides of the square; then will the parts of these diameters between the square and the outer circle represent the four apothems of the four slant sides of the pyramid. Connect the angles of the square with the circumference of the outer circle by lines at the four points indicated by the diameters, and the star of the pyramid is formed, which, when closed as a solid, will be a correct model of Cheops.

Calling apothem of Cheops, $MH = 34$
and half base, $HC = 21$
as per Figure 6. Then—$MH + MC = 55$

and $55 : 34 :: 34 : 21{\cdot}018$, being only in error a few inches in the pyramid itself, if carried into actual measures.

The ratio, therefore, of apothem to half-base, 34 to 21, which I ascribe to Cheops, is as near as stone and mortar can be got to illustrate the above proportions.

Correctly stated arithmetically let $MH = 2$.

Then $HC = \sqrt{5} - 1$
$MC = \sqrt{5} + 1$
and altitude of Cheops $= \sqrt{MH \times MC}$

Let us now compare the construction of the two stars :—

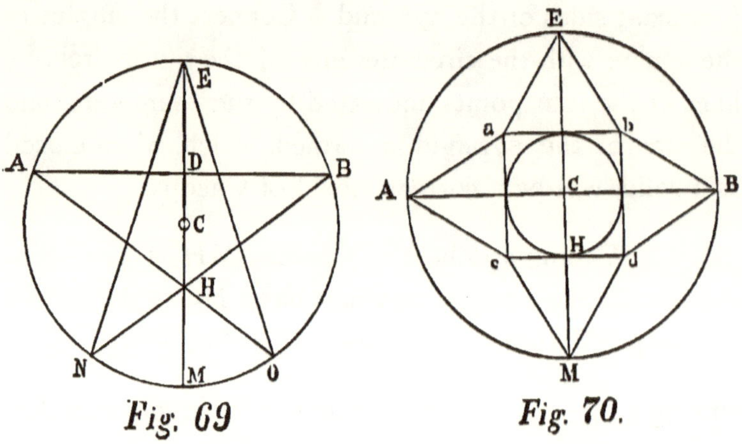

Fig. 69 *Fig.* 70.

TO CONSTRUCT THE STAR PENTALPHA FIG. 69.	TO CONSTRUCT THE STAR CHEOPS, FIG. 70.
Describe a circle. Draw diameter MCE. Divide MC in mean and extreme ratio at H. Lay off half MH from C, to D. Draw chord ADB, at right angles to diameter ECM. Draw chord BHN, through H. Draw chord AHO, through H. Connect NE. Connect EO.	Describe a circle. Draw diameter MCE. Divide MC in mean and extreme ratio, at H. Describe an inner circle with radius CH, and around it describe the square a, b, c, d. Draw diameter ACB, at right angles to diameter ECM. Draw Aa, aE, Eb, bB, Bd, dM, Mc, and cA.

The question now arises, does this pyramid Cheops set forth by the relations of its altitude to perimeter of base the ratio of diameter to circumference ; or, does it set forth mean proportional, and extreme and mean ratio, by the proportions of its apothem, altitude, and half-base ? The answer is—from the practical impossibility of such extreme accuracy in such a mass of masonry, that it points alike to all, and may as fairly be considered the exponent of the one as of the others. Piazzi Smyth makes Cheops 761·65 feet base, and 484·91 feet altitude, which is very nearly what he calls a π pyramid, for which I reckon the altitude would be about 484·87 feet with the same base: and for a pyramid of extreme and mean ratio the altitude would be 484·34 feet.

The whole difference, therefore, is only about six inches in a height of nearly five hundred feet. This difference, evidently beyond the power of man to discover, now that the pyramid is a ruin, would even in its perfect state have been inappreciable.

It appears most probable that the star Pentalpha led to the star Cheops, and that the star Cheops (*Fig.* 70) was the plan used by the ancient architect, and the ratio of 34 to 21, hypotenuse to base, the template used by the ancient builders.

Suppose some king said to his architect, "Make me a plan of a pyramid, of which the base shall be 420 cubits square, and altitude shall be to the perimeter of the base as the radius of a circle to the circumference." —Then might the architect prepare an elaborate plan in which the relative dimensions would be about—

R. B. CUBITS.

Base angle 51° 51′ 14·3″ { Base 420
Altitude . . . . 267·380304 &c.
Apothem . . . .339·988573 &c.

The king then orders another pyramid, of the same base, of which altitude is to be a mean proportional between apothem and half-base—and apothem and half-base taken as one line are to be in mean and extreme ratio.

The architect's plan of this pyramid will be the simple figure illustrated by me (*Fig.* 70), and the dimensions about—

R. B. CUBITS.

Base angle $51° 49' 37\frac{42}{471}''$ { Base 420
Altitude. . .267·1239849 &c.
Apothem. . 339·7875153 &c.

But the builder practically carries out *both* plans when he builds to my templates of 34 to 21 with—

R. B. CUBITS.

Base angle 51° 51′ 20″ { Base 420
Altitude . . .267·394839 &c.
Apothem . . 340

and neither king nor architect could detect error in the work.

The reader will remember that I have previously advanced that the level of Cephren's base was the plan level of the Gïzeh pyramids, and that at this level the base of Cheops measures 420 R.B. cubits—same as the base of Cephren.

This hypothesis is supported by the revelations of the pentangle, in which the ratio of 34 to 21 = apothem 340 to half-base 210 R.B. cubits, is so nearly approached.

Showing how proportional lines were the order of the pyramids of Gïzeh, we will summarise the proportions of the three main pyramids as shewn by my dimensions and ratios, very nearly, viz. :—

Mycerinus. Base : *Apothem* : : *Altitude* : *Half-Base.*

as shown by the ratios, (*Fig.* 13), 40 : 32 : : 25 : 20.

Cephren. Diagonal of Base : *Edge* : : *Edge* : *Altitude.*

as shown by ratios, (*Fig.* 12), 862 : 588 : : 588 : 400.

Cheops. (*Apothem* + *Half-Base*) : *Apoth.* : : *Apoth.* : *Half-Base.*

as shown by the ratios, (*Fig.* 9), 55 : 34 : : 34 : 21.

and—*Apothem* : *Altitude* : : *Altitude* : *Half-B.*

Similar close relations to other stars may be found in other pyramids. Thus :—*Suppose NHO of figure* 69 *to be the NHO of a heptangle instead of a pentangle,* then does NH represent apothem, and NO represent base of the pyramid Mycerinus, while the co-sine of the angle NHM (being MH minus versed sine) will be equal to the altitude of the pyramid. The angle NHM in the heptangle is, 38° 34′ 17·142″, and according to my plan of the pyramid Mycerinus, the corresponding angle is 38° 40′ 56″. (*See Fig.* 19.) This angular difference of 0° 6′ 39″ would only make a difference in the apothem of the pyramid of *eight inches*, and of *ten inches* in its altitude (apothem being 283 *ft.* 1 *inch*, and altitude 221 *ft.*).

§ 17. THE MANNER IN WHICH THE SLOPE RATIOS OF THE PYRAMIDS WERE ARRIVED AT.

The manner in which I arrived at the Slope Ratios of the Pyramids, viz., 32 *to* 20, 33 *to* 20, and 34 *to* 21, for *Mycerinus*, *Cephren*, and *Cheops*, respectively (*see Figures* 8, 7 *and* 6), was as follows:—

First, believing in the connection between the relative positions of the Pyramids on plan (*see Fig.* 3, 4 *or* 5), and their slopes, I viewed their positions thus:—

Mycerinus, situate at the angle of the 3, 4, 5 triangle ADC, is likely to be connected with that "primary" in his slopes.

Cephren, situate at the angle of the 20, 21, 29 triangle FAB, and strung, as it were, on the hypotenuse of the 3, 4, 5 triangle DAC, is likely to be connected with *both* primaries in his slopes.

Cheops, situate at the point A, common to both main triangles, governing the position of the other pyramids, is likely to be a sort of mean between these two pyramids in his slope ratios.

Reasoning thus, with the addition of the knowledge I possessed of the angular estimates of these slopes made by those who had visited the ground, and a useful start for my ratios gained by the reduction of base measures already known into R.B. cubits, giving 420 as a general base for Cheops and Cephren at one level, and taking 210 cubits as the base of Mycerinus (half the base of Cephren, as generally admitted), I had something solid and substantial to go upon. I commenced with Mycerinus. (*See Fig.* 71.)

(Mycerinus) Fig. 71.

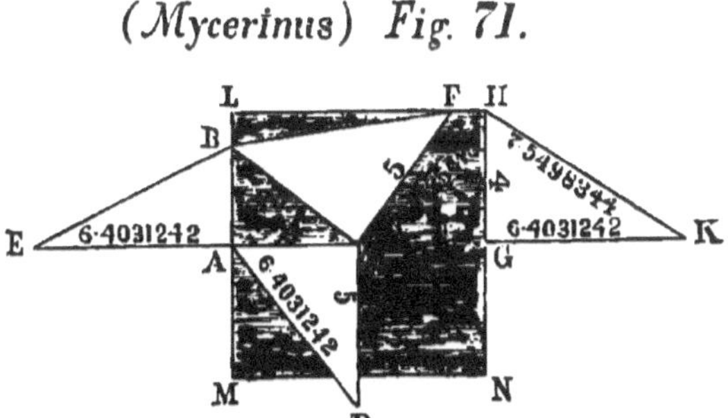

LHNM represents the base of the pyramid. On the half-base AC I described a 3, 4, 5 triangle ABC. I then projected the line CF = BC to be the altitude of the pyramid. Thus I erected the triangle BFC, ratio of BC to CF being 1 to 1. From this datum I arrived at the triangles BEA, ADC, and GKH. GK, EA, and AD, each represent apothem of pyramid; CF, and CD, altitude; and HK, edge.

The length of the line AD being $\sqrt{AC^2 + CD^2}$, the length of the line HK being $\sqrt{HG^2 + GK^2}$, and line CH (half diagonal of base) being $\sqrt{CG^2 + GH^2}$. These measures reduced to R.B. cubits, calling the line AC = ratio 4 = 105 cubits, half-base of pyramid, give the following results:—

	R. B. CUBITS.	BRITISH FEET.
Half-base ....LA =	105·000 =	176·925
Apothem ....EA =	168·082 =	283·218
Edge ....HK =	198·183 =	333·937
Altitude...........CD =	131·250 =	221·156
Half diag. of base..CH =	148·4924 =	250·209

and thus I acquired the ratios :—

Half-base : Altitude : : Apothem : Base.

= 20 : 25 : : 32 : 40 nearly.

To place the lines of the diagram in their actual solid position—Let AB, BC, CA and HG be hinges attaching the planes AEB, BFC, CDA and HKG to the base LHNM. Lift the plane BCF on its hinge till the point F is vertical over the centre C. Lift plane CDA on its hinge, till point D is vertical over the centre C; then will line CD touch CF, and become one line. Now lift the plane AEB on its hinge, until point E is vertical over the centre C, and plane HKG on its hinge till point K is vertical over the centre C; then will points E, F, D and K, all meet at one point above the centre C, and all the lines will be in their proper places.

The angle at the base of Mycerinus, if built to a ratio of 4 to 5 (half-base to altitude), and not to the more practical but nearly perfect ratio of 32 to 20 (apothem to half-base) would be the complement of angle ADC, thus—

$$\frac{4}{5} = \cdot 8 = \text{Tan.} \angle ADC = 38^\circ\ 39'\ 35\tfrac{165}{477}''$$

$$\therefore \angle DAC = 51^\circ\ 20'\ 24\tfrac{312}{477}''$$

but as it is probable that the pyramid was built to the ratio of 32 to 20, I have shown its base angle in Figure 19, as 51° 19′ 4″.

Figure 72 shows how the slopes of *Cephren* were arrived at.

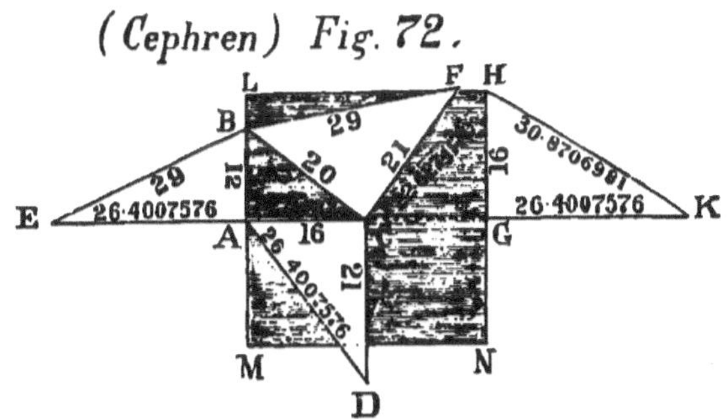

(*Cephren*) *Fig.* 72.

LHNM represents the base of the pyramid. On the half-base AC, I described a 3, 4, 5 triangle ABC. I then projected the line CF (ratio 21 to BC 20), thus erecting the 20, 21, 29 triangle BCF. From this datum, I arrived at the triangles BEA, ADC, and GKH; GK, EA and AD each representing apothem; CF and CD, altitude; and HK, edge. The lengths of the lines AD, HK and CH being got at as in the pyramid Mycerinus. These measures reduced to cubits, calling AC = ratio 16 = 210 cubits (half-base of pyramid) give the following result.

	R. B. CUBITS.	BRITISH FEET.
Half-base, ...	210·00	......353·85 = LA
Apothem.	346·50	......583·85 = EA
Edge	405·16	......682·69 = HK
Altitude	275·625	......464·43 = CD
Half-diag. of base	296·985	......500·42 = CH

thus I get the ratios of—Apothem : Half-Base : : 33 : 20, &c. The planes in the diagram are placed in their correct positions, as directed for Figure 71.

The angle at the base of Cephren, if built to the ratio of 16 to 21 (half-base to altitude), and not to the practical ratio of 33 to 20 (apothem to half-base), would be the complement of < ADC, thus—

$$\frac{16}{21} = \cdot 761904 = \text{Tan.} < ADC = 37^\circ\ 18'\ 14\tfrac{16}{46}''$$
$$\therefore \qquad < DAC = 52^\circ\ 41'\ 45''\tfrac{30}{46}$$

but as it is probable that the pyramid was built to the ratio of 33 to 20, I have marked the base angle in Fig. 17, as 52° 41′ 41″.

I took *Cheops* out, first as a π pyramid, and made his lines to a base of 420 cubits, as follows—

Half-base 210
Altitude 267.380304
Apothem . . . . 339.988573 (*See Fig.* 73.)

(Cheops) Fig. 73.

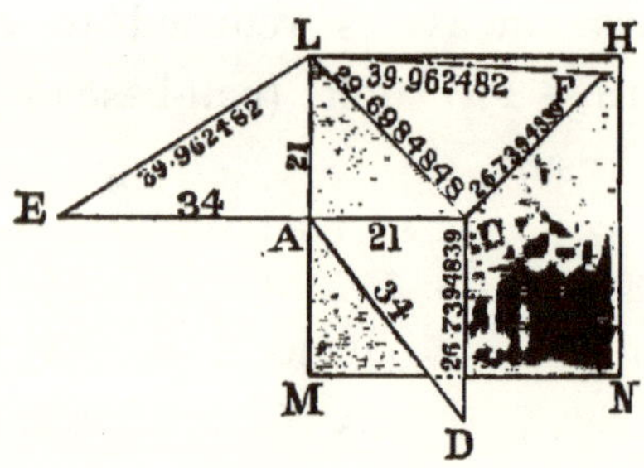

But to produce the building ratio of 34 to 21, as per diagram Figure 6 or 9, I had to alter it to—

Half-base 210
Altitude . . . . 267·394839
Apothem 340

Thus the theoretical angle of Cheops is 51° 51′ 14·3″, and the probable angle at which it was built is 51° 51′ 20″, as per figure 15.

Cheops is therefore the mean or centre of a system—the slopes of Mycerinus being a little flatter, and those of Cephren a little steeper, Cheops coming fairly between the two, within about 10 minutes; and thus the connection between the ground plan of the group and the slopes of the three pyramids is exactly as one might expect after examination of Figure 3, 4 or 5.

www.ingramcontent.com/pod-product-compliance
Lightning Source LLC
Chambersburg PA
CBHW032017010726
47493CB00007B/2447

* 9 7 8 3 3 3 7 4 0 5 9 8 4 *